"Pat? Are you decent?" Dusty asked softly.

"Always."

"I mean, can I come in?"

"You can go anywhere you want. You own the building, remember?"

"Pat, stop fooling around, I meant, are you dressed to receive guests?"

His shaggy brown head peeked around the door. There were beads of water on his forehead and his hair was wet. "It depends on the guests. You, I would receive anytime."

Dusty shook her head and sighed. He was impossible! "I am just asking how much of your naked body I'll see if I go in there."

"How much do you want to see?"

Oh, why hadn't she gotten a guard dog like some of her neighbors?

Then Pat stepped from behind the door. "Is this enough?"

He wore a pair of jogging shorts and nothing else. Dusty fought to keep from staring at him. Pat's glistening body looked magnificent, she thought, dazed.

"Not enough?" His tone was teasing.

She found her voice at last. "Enough . . ."

WHAT ARE *LOVESWEPT* ROMANCES?

They are stories of true romance and touching emotion. We believe those two very important ingredients are constants in our highly sensual and very believable stories in the *LOVESWEPT* line. Our goal is to give you, the reader, stories of consistently high quality that may sometimes make you laugh, sometimes make you cry, but are always fresh and creative and contain many delightful surprises within their pages.

Most romance fans read an enormous number of books. Those they truly love, they keep. Others may be traded with friends and soon forgotten. We hope that each *LOVESWEPT* romance will be a treasure—a "keeper." We will always try to publish

LOVE STORIES YOU'LL NEVER FORGET
BY AUTHORS YOU'LL ALWAYS REMEMBER

The Editors

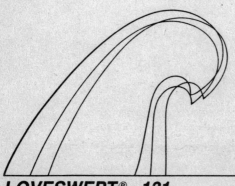

LOVESWEPT® • 131

Anne and Ed Kolaczyk
The Butler and His Lady

 BANTAM BOOKS
TORONTO • NEW YORK • LONDON • SYDNEY • AUCKLAND

THE BUTLER AND HIS LADY
A Bantam Book / March 1986

LOVESWEPT® and the wave device are registered
trademarks of Bantam Books, Inc. Registered in U.S. Patent
and Trademark Office and elsewhere.

ISBN 0-553-21745-3

Published simultaneously in the United States and Canada

Bantam Books are published by Bantam Books, Inc. Its
trademark, consisting of the words "Bantam Books" and
the portrayal of a rooster, is Registered in U.S. Patent and
Trademark Office and in other countries. Marca Registrada.
Bantam Books, Inc., 666 Fifth Avenue, New York, New
York 10103.

PRINTED IN THE UNITED STATES OF AMERICA

O   0 9 8 7 6 5 4 3 2 1

To the dear friends of Patrick Mahoney
who made this little bit of immortality possible

One

Camilla Ross felt terrible. Her head hurt, her throat was sore, and her whole body ached. Every time she coughed, her chest was wracked with pain.

"Why don't you go home?" her boss asked her early in the afternoon.

"I'm fine," she insisted. "And I have to get the paperwork started on the Tilden Lake deal. Buyers for two-million-dollar office complexes don't grow on trees. I want to get the papers signed as soon as possible."

"The title search will take at least five days," he pointed out. "Get Jessica started on the paperwork, then go home. Spread any more of your germs around here and you'll wipe out the whole office."

"I certainly wouldn't want to do that." A spasm of coughing stopped her from saying anything more and left her feeling light-headed and weak. Dusty might be her nickname, but it certainly wasn't how she felt at the moment. Drippy was more like it. Or Dizzy. Decrepit. Depressed.

Her decision made before she really knew it, Dusty got to her feet and quickly sorted through the papers on her desk. Most were put aside for later filing; the rest were tossed into her briefcase. The image of a bowl of soup floated into her head as she crossed the tile floor of the work area to get her coat. Hot soup with steam dancing above it, beckoning her with its comforting warmth.

She held on to the soothing thought as she rode the elevator downstairs and hurried outside to hail a cab. It was late February and the weather was a miserable combination of snow and rain. Dusty's body shivered, but her mind kept whispering, "Soup, soup, soup."

It was only as her cab was speeding north along Lake Michigan that the hot soup spilled and turned to ice. Her kitchen was as empty as Mother Hubbard's cupboard, she remembered with an inner groan. She had planned to go grocery shopping last weekend, but hadn't quite gotten around to it.

Once they turned off Lake Shore Drive, Dusty leaned forward, "Pull into the parking lot of that grocery store, will you? I've got to get a few things."

The white-haired cab driver glared into his mirror at her. "The meter, she got to run." He pointed to the taxi meter. The Caribbean sunshine in the man's lilting tones had no effect on either the overcast sky or her mood.

"Yes, I know."

"She maybe run long time."

"I don't care. I'll pay you even if I'm inside a week." She got out of the cab and hurried toward the store.

"Hey, lady." The driver's voice caught up with her

before she got very far. "You get me candy bar, okay? Hershey, with nuts. Big bar. Okay?"

She nodded agreement and stepped into the relative warmth of the store. She was probably the only person in Chicago who had cab drivers asking her for candy bars. What was it about her small frame that made people assume she'd be happy to do them favors? Or maybe they thought she'd be too timid to refuse. Wasn't that part of her problem in finding a housekeeper? Everyone but her clients viewed her as a pushover.

She bought her groceries, and then lugged them back to the cab. The cold air penetrated her coat, slid under her sweater, and lay damply against her skin. She felt awful.

"You got my candy bar, lady?"

Dusty handed it to him without a word.

"Many thanks." He broke off a piece for himself and held the package out to her. "You want some, lady?"

The smell of the rich chocolate made her feel worse, if that were possible. "No, thank you," she said vehemently. "Just get me home."

"Sure thing, lady."

He gunned the cab's motor and slewed out into the street without looking for pedestrians or cars. Dusty shut her eyes and prayed, feeling the cab swaying around corners and hearing the protesting squeal of the tires. Then the cab jolted to a stop, and she clutched at her groceries to keep them from scattering. Her purse fell to the floor. They were parked in front of the two-story brownstone she owned.

"Fast enough, lady?"

She handed him a ten-dollar bill and opened the door, escaping into the icy rain. "Keep the change."

The man leaped around to take her grocery bag and

carried it to the front door. "You want I put these away?"

"No, thank you." She took the bag from his hands and went inside. Maybe he'd like to hire on as her housekeeper. Unfortunately he probably earned more driving a cab.

After dumping the contents of her mailbox into the grocery bag, she climbed the newly carpeted stairs to her second-floor apartment. The building, her first personal venture into real estate, made her feel that she wasn't doing too badly at all for a twenty-nine-year-old ex-secretary only halfway to her bachelor's degree. Her apartment alone was bigger than the Canaryville bungalow she'd grown up in, and then there were two one-bedroom units on the first floor and a garden apartment in the English basement.

Dusty balanced her grocery bag in one arm and unlocked the two dead bolts on her door. Then, steeling herself, she forced her eyes to survey what was visible of the apartment. It was a mess, but the same mess she had left that morning. Her breath escaped in a quick sigh and she entered, slamming and bolting the heavy steel door behind her.

The low purchase price of the building had been a plus, but the location was still a slight negative. It was a few blocks beyond the outer edge of the area that was undergoing renovation.

She'd known the risks when she bought it, but that hadn't prepared her for the emotional trauma of a burglary. Crime was supposed to occur only on TV or to other people. It had happened over three months ago, but she still grew tense when she came home to the large empty apartment. If only she could find a live-in housekeeper.

Dusty carried the groceries into the kitchen and

shoved aside two weeks' worth of junk mail and an empty cereal box to make room on the counter for the bags. Suddenly the effort of making dinner just wasn't worth it. The heck with the soup.

She swallowed two aspirin with a glass of orange drink and went into her bedroom, stretching out on the unmade bed. It felt so good to lie down. She kicked her shoes off and pulled a corner of the blanket over her, sinking into the pillows.

It wasn't as if she were looking for the impossible— just someone to do light cleaning, make breakfast and dinner, and run some errands. Mostly what she wanted was someone to fill up a few of the empty spaces, but the last woman the agency had sent over was eighty if she was a day and could barely make it up the stairs. The younger ones didn't like the neighborhood, the color scheme of the kitchen, or the salary.

Dusty snuggled farther under the blanket, some of the aches and chills subsiding. The aspirin were starting to work, but as the general discomfort of her body lessened, the gnawing in her stomach increased. Its empty growling reminded her that she hadn't eaten anything all day but coffee and aspirin.

In just a few more minutes she'd get up and make that hot soup, but the pillow fit around her so seductively and kept pulling her toward a pleasant, gentle land, a warm, sunshiny land filled with little elves who promised to take her weariness in trade for vim and vigor. . . .

The ringing of the phone signaled her expulsion from that magic land. The elves slammed the gate shut, throwing Dusty back to earth. "Damn," she muttered, and fumbled for the phone.

"Dusty?" A disgustingly cheerful voice bubbled

into her ear from the receiver. "This is Maggie Lucas at the Ascot Agency. I've found the ideal candidate for your housekeeping position."

Candidate? Was she hiring a housekeeper or electing one? Dusty shook her head in an effort to clear it. "Does the candidate speak English?"

"With a touch of the brogue." Maggie laughed. "The only thing is—"

"Did you discuss the salary I can afford?"

"No problem."

"How about the neighborhood?"

The woman laughed heartily. "Pat Mahoney isn't about to let something like that worry—"

"Fine." Vertical was not Dusty's best position at the moment, and conversation was not her best skill. The room tilted precariously. "Can she get here in an hour for an interview?"

Maggie Lucas annoyingly hearty laughter pealed out again. "No problem there, Dusty, except—"

"Good." Dusty slammed down the phone and reclaimed the pillow, closing her eyes briefly to fight off dizziness.

When her head had stopped spinning, Dusty gingerly focused her eyes on her digital bedside clock. She'd been asleep about three hours. The returning ache in her head and joints told her that the aspirin was wearing off. She sat up and found that the dizziness had been replaced by nausea. It was just as well she hadn't had that soup.

Ignoring the pillow's beckoning and its promises of sweet sleep and peaceful dreams, Dusty jerked herself up. No little flu bug was going to keep her down.

Springing into action, she made the bed, toying briefly with the idea of changing the sheets. By the time she had finished, though, most of her energy had disappeared, and she decided to spend what was left of her waning strength in the living area.

Her visit to the kitchen was brief. One look into the grocery bag was enough to remind her stomach of its emptiness and she chose to tackle the dining room instead. The clutter was even worse in the living room, and she sank onto a sofa, kicking a black leather pump out of her way.

What was she doing? She was the one hiring at this interview, not the other way around. If she had the time and energy to pick up after herself, she wouldn't need a housekeeper. She worked hard selling commercial real estate and deserved a rest when she came home. There wasn't any reason to feel guilty or intimidated.

For the past nine years she'd paid her dues at Putney and Bowkers, starting as a clerk and rising through the ranks to a position as one of their top salespeople. Sheer determination and hard work had earned her success, not a college degree or nepotism. Now she was starting to reap some of the benefits of that success, and she'd have to learn to relax and enjoy them. Even if she had to force herself.

The silent mocking of the clutter finally got to her and she turned upon it with a vengeance. No use frightening Ms. Mahoney out of her wits the minute she stepped through the door. Once the place was cleaned, it wouldn't be hard to maintain. The apartment was cluttered, not really dirty.

Dusty scurried about picking up shoes, stockings, and belts, slippers, scarves, and a sweater. Everything was thrown into her bedroom closet to be tended to later, when she was feeling stronger. With luck, Ms. Mahoney would start work next Monday and that would give Dusty the weekend to straighten up the place.

After hiding most of the clutter she wiped a kitchen towel over the dustiest of the flat surfaces. The rainy skies were actually a blessing. Sun filtering in through that large bay window would have spotlighted the dust. This way, it was discreetly hidden.

By three forty-five the apartment was presentable, Dusty had taken a quick shower and was dressed in a pair of jeans and a pink sweatshirt. Not the most authoritative-looking ensemble, but better than the flannel nightgown she'd been longing for. She tied her shoulder-length reddish-brown hair back with a green ribbon, and practiced a steely-eyed look of control.

Satisfied that she was ready to take charge right from the beginning, she went into the living room. The floor seemed to tilt a bit to the left, and she used the walls to get herself over to the sofa. She was just about to sit down when the buzzer sounded. By the time she worked her way over to the intercom, the ringing in her ears would have rivaled any doorbell.

"Miss Ross? This is Pat Mahoney."

Either it was the ringing in her ears, or Ms. Mahoney had one heck of a cold. Maybe they could trade germs.

"Come on up," Dusty said.

It didn't seem worth the effort to cross the room again, so she leaned against the wall, eyes closed, until the rap came at the door a few moments later. She swung the door open.

"Come in, Ms. Maho—"

The balance of her greeting froze in Dusty's throat as she stared at the tall, husky man standing in the doorway. He appeared to be in his late thirties, and a broad, devilish smile danced across his face as he took a step into the room.

"You're not Ms. Mahoney," she croaked.

"Not since the last time I checked."

His voice was deep with a musical lilt to it that almost hid its strength. His broad grin seemed to grow more menacing. Icy fingers of fear gripped Dusty's throat. Why were those blue eyes twinkling? What fiendish things did he have in mind for her?

"If you leave now, I won't call the police." She tried to force sternness into her voice, but the floor chose that moment to wobble and she had to grab the edge of a credenza to steady herself.

"What?"

He wasn't smiling anymore and the single step he took toward her intensified the cold fear squeezing Dusty's lungs. She couldn't breathe. She could feel her mouth move, but no sound came out as she plunged into a whirlpool of total darkness.

Pat caught the woman before she hit the floor and carried her into the living room. She was a light little thing, both of body and light-headed, it seemed. Why had she let him in and then started to talk about calling the police? He put her down on the sofa, took off her shoes, and loosened the belt on her jeans.

Damn. He'd been hoping this would work out too. The way the agency had described it, the job would have fit him to a "T." Career woman who needed a little light houskeeping and looking after. Room, board, a few pennies for a glass of brew now and then, and a lot of free time so he could get his own project on its feet.

He spent a moment staring down into the woman's

pale face. Her lashes, almost lost in the shadows beneath her eyes, didn't move. With a sigh of resignation for the wasted afternoon, he took off his raincoat and tossed it on a chair, then went in search of the kitchen. Luckily he had a sturdy heart, for it looked like a battlefield. His mum used to say that seeing a woman's kitchen was like seeing into her mind. That didn't bode well for Miss Ross's mental state.

After some searching through the debris he found a cloth, which he dampened and used to wipe her face but she showed no signs of coming around. He hoped she hadn't taken some kind of weird substance. Americans seemed to like to experiment a lot, whereas his countrymen were satisfied to drink the same grog with which they'd greeted St. Patrick. "Damn," he said aloud softly as the notion occurred to him that she might be seriously ill.

Pat dampened the cloth again, cooler water this time. He'd try once more to bring her around and then he was going to call the paramedics. He couldn't afford to get mixed up in the problems of a strange woman.

When the agency had told him of the job, he'd pictured Miss Ross as a brisk woman in her thirties, on the ball and on the go. Ready to take charge or lead a charge. Not someone needing a nursemaid. He placed the cool cloth across her forehead and her eyes flew open. Terror-stricken, she looked like a big-eyed doe trapped by hunting dogs.

"Why are you still here?"

"It's my mother's doing, God rest her soul," he said gently, hoping to calm her enough so that he could leave. "She made me into such a gentleman that I could never ignore a lady in distress."

Pat slowly backed over to a chair and sat down as

the woman sat up gingerly, the damp cloth falling to the sofa unnoticed as her hands strayed to her waist. The fear in her eyes intensified.

"What did you do to me?"

"You fainted—"

"My shoes," she whispered hoarsely, now staring down at her bare feet. "Where are they?"

"I took them off. You—"

"I have a whole closet full of shoes. If you promise to leave right away, I'll let you have all of them."

Pat got to his feet and started for the door. Chivalry was one thing, but this lady was beyond strange. Her face was no longer pale, but rosy with an almost too-healthy glow, and her eyes glittered.

"Would you like me to call the paramedics?" he asked. "Or do you have a family physician you'd prefer?"

"Why?" She sounded close to tears. "What did you do to me?"

That was it. He'd seen the kitchen; there was no reasoning with a mind like hers. "Lady," he snapped. "If I did anything to you, the joyous memories would last you a lifetime. Maybe two."

Confusion swam in her eyes. "You're a strange man. What do you want?"

"*I'm* strange?" His short fuse flared and ignited his temper. "You should talk. I come here for an interview and you treat me as if I'm from the Genghis Khan agency."

"Interview?" She looked bewildered and tried to get to her feet. The rosy hue in her cheeks vanished, leaving almost no color at all.

His mother's presence blocked his way to the door. She wouldn't let him leave this woman in the state she was in. "You don't look too good."

"Most people don't look too good when they have the flu."

Some of his apprehension faded, replaced quickly by remorse for misjudging her. Poor thing, no wonder she was acting so strangely. A different type of apprehension grew in its place. Since when was he interested in the mother-hen role? "Do you have anybody to come here and stay with you?"

"I don't need anybody. I'm a big girl and I can take care of myself."

Her determination to be independent increased his reluctance to leave. "Right. Just the same, I'll check out the kitchen. You look like you haven't eaten in a while. I'll see what I can throw together."

Ignoring the war being waged between cleanliness and clutter, he looked through the refrigerator and the cabinets. There was little food on hand, and all of it was atrocious. No wonder she was sick if she ate all this junk. This little lady needed someone to take care of her.

Pat refused to acknowledge the blaring alarm that went off in his brain. He'd just put together a few bites, get the little bird sitting up, and then'd he'd be off, faster than a fox in the hunt season.

"You eat out a lot, don't you?" he called to her.

"Yes, I do."

She sounded tired. The best thing for her would be a bowl of hot soup and an early bedtime.

"Look, Mr. Mahoney. I came home early from work to rest and then the agency called about you. Mrs. Lucas called you Pat, and I thought— I'm really quite tired. Could you leave, please?"

He paid no attention to her feeble protests and stepped into the doorway with a package of powdered soup. "Do you really eat this stuff?"

"It's quick."

So was arsenic. He tried not to shudder, guessing it was better than nothing. He found a pot and heated some water. The stuff didn't smell like his soup, but it would warm her up. He carried the cup into the living room.

"This will make you feel a little better until I can get some real food into the house. I'll buy some stuff to make a hot toddy too. That's the best way to cure colds and flu."

"I can make my own. I have whiskey, sugar, and water."

"Sugar," Pat scoffed. "The white death. You need honey and lemon. Pure lemon. Not the junk that sits around in a bottle on a grocer's shelf."

"I just wish you'd go, Mr. Mahoney. This whole thing is one big mistake."

"Don't worry about it, we all make mistakes."

"But—" Her voice wasn't strong enough to carry down the hallway as he walked along it past the kitchen. He found her bedroom, took the pillows off the bed, and carried them out to the living room to put them under her head. Then he went back and got an extra blanket out of the closet, noting the pile of shoes on the floor. His mother hadn't offered any advice about closets.

"You've got a big place here. It took me a while to find the blanket."

She just lay there with her eyes closed, looking like a little girl home from school.

Poor thing, she must be really rundown. He stood up and went back into the kitchen, where he had seen her purse. He rumaged through it until he found a set of keys and then brought them back into the living room.

"These your house keys?"

"Mr. Mahoney," she began.

"Just call me Pat. House keys, yes or no?"

She nodded mutely.

"Okay," he said, and put on his raincoat. "I've got a lot of shopping to do, so you just relax."

She glared at him, and Pat couldn't help smiling. She was such a cute little lassie.

"Here, I'll put something nice on for you." He flipped the TV channels through the afternoon cartoon shows. "Lord bless us, that mouse is spitting on the cat. These are much too violent." He continued turning the channels. "Ah, Mister Rogers. That's a good one for you."

Pat turned, pleased with his choice, but Miss Ross was frowning as much as that cat had been. If she were a cartoon character, there'd be smoke coming out of her ears. It must be the fever. "Now, don't let anybody in unless you know them. You seem a little careless about that." He closed the door carefully behind him and locked it with the key.

This job might work out after all, he decided, ignoring the little voice that warned him he was already too attracted by this woman's vulnerability. Miss Ross seemed reasonable, the apartment wouldn't be hard to manage, and he even liked the neighborhood. It reminded him of the part of Liverpool he and his family had lived in during the good times. The houses here didn't have the same age and history behind them, but they had charm, and the smorgasbord of residents added character. It felt like home already.

Two

_____

The muscled giant swooped Dusty up in his arms. She held on tightly, wrapping one arm around his neck and laying the other across his broad shoulder. His body was hard steel cables covered by rough skin; a vibrant, animal energy pulsed through his frame. He was a wild Irish warrior and she was his prize.

He carried her through the dense forest toward his lair, and she knew he wanted her and was going to make her his own. An answering desire surged through her. The intensity of his deep blue eyes increased, and she knew they were getting closer. Closer to ecstasy.

She squirmed slightly as his powerful arms tightened around her, but the more she squirmed, the tighter they became, and she began to panic. They were too tight. She didn't want to be held like that. She needed freedom to give her love fully. She struggled even more, moaning with desire and the need to be free.

"Miss Ross, are you all right?"

Dusty's eyes flew open. The muscular giant was shaking her lightly and a disappointed moan escaped her lips. He had gotten dressed.

"Are you all right? You were crying out and I was afraid something was wrong," Pat said. "Maybe it was just a bad dream."

Dusty's mind slowly began to function. "Yes, it was just a bad dream." She freed herself from the tangle of sheets and blankets that had imprisoned her, the imagined passion still tingling through her body. She hoped she hadn't called out anything intelligible. Her cheeks reddened at the thought.

"Now that you're awake, shall I fix breakfast? Something light perhaps, some poached eggs and muffins?"

"Yes, fine." She swung her feet out of bed as she glanced at her clock. It was nine-thirty. "Oh, Lord, I'm late. I won't have time for breakfast."

"Sure, you will." Pat was disappearing around the doorway into the hall, and his words drifted back to her. "You aren't going to work today."

"What do you mean I'm not going to work?" Silence was her only reply. "Pat!"

She hurried after him and collided with a solid wall of Irish masculinity in the doorway. His arms reached out to keep her from falling, but even after she had regained her balance they remained around her.

"Yes, ma'am?"

Dusty swallowed once to calm herself and took a step back. Out of his arms.

"What do you mean I'm not going to work?"

"Oh, your secretary called and I told her you were

still a bit under the weather. She just called back and said all of today's appointments have been rescheduled."

"I see." She readily admitted she wasn't up to full speed yet, but missing work was her decision to make. She wanted a houseman/butler not a father. This wasn't going to work out.

"I also must confess to causing a slight misunderstanding last night," he went on. "A gentleman named Ron wanted to speak to Dusty and unfortunately he had to call back several times before he thought to tell me it was you." His glance was slightly scolding. "The agency said your name was Camilla."

Ron! She had forgotten all about him! "Why didn't you wake me?"

"I'm not sure I could have. You were visiting with the angels."

If she had been, it was only because of those hot toddies of his. She rushed back into her bedroom. How could she have convinced herself last night that a butler would be much better than a housekeeper? It had been his dancing blue eyes and the easy way those hot toddies went down.

"Breakfast in a half hour?" Pat called after her.

"Fine."

She picked up the phone and dialed quickly. "Ron," she said before he could finish his greeting. "It's Dusty. I'm really sorry about last night. I was sick and just forgot we had a date."

Ron's voice was not sympathetic. "Who was the guy I spoke to?"

"My butler."

"Butler? He sounded more like a bouncer in a West Side bar."

She felt Ron's disapproval surround her like yesterday's cold rain and she knew she had made another mistake. Ron was born knowing whom to hire and whom not to, while she was grateful to find anybody willing to work for her. So what if Pat was strong, gentle, and gorgeous? He still didn't suit her needs. She ignored the memories rushing over her. A fever-induced dream was no reason to hire someone either.

"Well, he's not going to be around much longer," she assured Ron. "He's not at all what I had in mind for the job." She paused. "Why don't you come here for dinner Friday?"

"Are you cooking?"

"I can broil steaks, you know."

"Maybe you'd better keep the butler through dinner Friday. I've got a big tennis game Saturday morning and I don't play my best after a bout with ptomaine."

"I've never poisoned you."

"Just luck, I guess. See you Friday."

Dusty hung up her phone with a sigh. Of all the men she'd dated over the last few years, Ron was the top. He took her to exclusive places, introduced her to influential people, but, best of all, their schedules were compatible. Her night-school classes on Tuesdays and Thursdays presented no problem because those were his racquetball nights, and she could work late on Mondays because he did too. They got along perfectly.

Satisfied that she had undone some of Pat's damage, she took a leisurely bubble bath, then got under the shower to wash her hair and rinse away her irritations. She dressed in slacks and an oxford-cloth shirt. She hadn't had Ron's experience with house servants, but she guessed that one did not fire them wearing only a flannel nightgown.

"Two minutes."

Dusty heard the call from the kitchen as she turned off her blow dryer and quickly tied her hair back with a ribbon. She slipped on her penny loafers without socks, and checked herself in the full-length mirror in her dressing room. She looked just right, she thought: informal, yet somewhat severe, perfect for establishing just who was in charge.

She glanced nervously at the clock. Her two minutes were almost up and she hurried out of the bedroom. Outside in the hall she brought herself up short. Why was she rushing around at his command? She was going to fire him. She slowed to a measured, dignified walk and entered the kitchen.

"Good morning, Miss Ross." The words rumbled up from his chest as if in song. "It's a good thing the flowers aren't blooming yet. One look at you and they'd pull back into the ground and quit."

"Thank you, Pat." Her lips pressed themselves into a tight straight line. The Blarney Stone probably had to kiss *his* lips to get its powers.

He seated her at the table, where a single red rose resided in a vase in the center and a copy of *The Wall Street Journal* awaited her at the place mat.

"I bought a fresh cantaloupe this morning," he told her, placing a wedge of the fruit, garnished with fresh strawberries, before her. "I hope you like it."

"I'm sure it'll be fine." The melon smelled fresh and sweet and reminded her of summer. She scooped out a spoonful and let it linger in her mouth. It was delicious.

Pat came to her side, a solid bulky presence in his dark trousers, white shirt, and black bow tie. Her previously spacious kitchen seemed to shrink around him. "I'm afraid I don't know your tastes yet, my lady. Would you prefer orange or peach marmalade?"

Dusty paused a moment as she stared intently at a line in *The Wall Street Journal*. Why was he standing so close? Bits of her dream kept replaying annoyingly in her mind. "Orange," she said finally without looking up.

He moved away and she went back to breathing and eating the melon. Maybe she should keep him around for a few days so that she could learn how to manage a butler. Her jaw clenched firmly. No. He was going. Right after breakfast. But she would give him a week's pay.

She tried to read her paper while she ate, but her mind kept returning to the night before like a piece of flotsam washing back up on the shore with each wave. When did she actually hire Pat? What were the terms?

She remembered his coming back from shopping, a strong, safe presence that filled the empty old apartment with warmth. She had dozed happily, awakening to a hot toddy made with honey and freshly squeezed lemon juice. Later she had his chicken soup: thick, rich, and filled with vegetables and meat. It had tasted so good, just what her weakened body had needed. Guilt pushed the flotsam farther up on the beach. She'd give him two week's severance pay.

After dinner he had made some more hot toddies. No. That sounded like more than one. He had made her one more.

"Finished, madam?"

She looked up and smiled. His blue eyes were warm, his voice soothing, and she felt the power of his hot toddies again. "Yes, thank you." It might have been two after all.

"Poached eggs, madam." He placed the plate in front of her.

After the second hot toddy he had drawn her bath. It had been just right, and she had lain in it and perspired, feeling all the germs being washed away. Then he had helped her prepare for bed.

Her cheeks glowed with warmth at the image of his undressing her. He hadn't really helped. He had just laid out her flannel nightgown and turned down her bed. As she changed he tidied up the bathroom.

She began to eat her eggs. He probably deserved a month's severance pay, but she had no problem with that.

"Coffee, madam?"

She started. "Yes, please." Then she painfully cleared her throat. "There are some things we'll have to discuss, Pat."

"Yes, I know: salary, which day off." He nodded with a gentle smile. "But why don't you go into the living room and relax first? I'll bring your coffee in to you. By the time I'm finished with the breakfast dishes and changing your bed, you'll be finished with your paper."

Dusty finished her eggs and trudged into the living room. By the time Pat was done with his chores, Dusty had finished her newspaper and had rehearsed her dismissal speech four times. She would be gracious, kind, and understanding. And firm. When he came in she motioned for him to take the chair across from her. That was a bad move. He was bigger and seemed closer than she had planned, and that twinkle in his eye was definitely not in her script. No matter though. She could handle it.

"Did you like the soup last night?" he asked before

she could get started. "I thought maybe you'd like the rest of it with a salad for lunch."

"The soup was delicious, Pat, but I'm afraid this just isn't going to work out."

The twinkle dimmed. "What's not?"

She had every right to dismiss him. She was not going to feel guilty. "When I asked Mrs. Lucas to find me a housekeeper, you weren't what I had in mind."

He nodded slowly, looking like a little boy who had lost his bike, his dog, and his best friend.

"You must see how awkward it is, the two of us living alone here." She suddenly felt worse than a murderess. What if he really needed this job? Maybe he was supporting a sick mother or a widowed sister and her four young children.

The gleam reappeared. "It'll be spring soon. Warm enough for me to sleep on the roof."

Little boy, hell! The only thing he was likely to be supporting was a string of girlfriends!

"Or if it gets too cold," he said, "I can sleep in the hallway. I promise not to molest your tenants, unless they want me to." The gleam had grown into a full-fledged laugh.

She was not going to let his amusement cow her. She was in charge here and she was making the decisions. "People will get the wrong idea about us."

His smile was understanding and tinged with sympathy. "That Ron who called? He's your boyfriend?"

"He has nothing to do with our present discussion."

"He didn't sound too pleased last night," Pat noted. "Have you had other handsome young . . . butlers?"

The grin on his face transferred the heat from Dusty's cheeks to her temper. She took a deep breath and let it out slowly to gain control of herself. "Ron is secure in our relationship," she said. "We share too many intellectual interests for him to be threatened by the physical presence of someone else."

Of their own volition her eyes seemed to linger on his bulging biceps. She forced herself to look away, but her gaze didn't find his face easier to rest on. His eyes were serious and still. Her conscience pricked her.

"I'm sorry if I offended you," she said. "I didn't mean that you were all brawn and no brain. I'm sure that—"

"No, no," he hastily assured her. "I wasn't thinking of myself at all. I was concerned about you. All this intellectualism without any physical activity isn't good for you. Your body needs stimulating as well as your mind."

"My body's stimulation is none of your business," she told him. His grin deepened but she refused to react to it. "I was merely pointing out why Ron would not be worried."

"Then I don't see the problem," Pat said. "You're happy with Ron and he won't feel threatened by me. If you're worried about me, you needn't be. A butler doesn't get involved."

Dusty's lips pursed. He had neatly disposed of all her arguments. She'd look like a fool, or a liar, if she harped anymore on the unsuitability of the arrangement.

"It sounds like we're safe to me," Pat pointed out.

"Yes, it does," she noted carefully, and picked her newspaper back up as he left the room. She'd decided to fire him and she would. But not right now.

Once Pat was gone she gave up any pretense of reading the paper and slid down into a reclining position. She would have been strong enough to go to work, but as long as she was home, she might as well let the sleep tugging at her take over. She'd worry about Pat later.

She was floating along on a warm cloud of peace when fear clutched at her, and her eyes snapped open. What had happened? She sat up, trying to shake the drowsiness away. Had the fear been part of her dream? A murmur of voices came through the front door and she heard the rattling of keys being tried. She was being robbed again.

"Pat," she screamed, and jumped to her feet. Should she call the police? Find a weapon? Hide?

Pat came rushing from the kitchen just as the door flew open. His husky frame took a challenging stance, his hands curved into fists. "What the hell do you want, buddy?" he snarled.

"What the hell's it to you, buddy?" The short, bulky, gray-haired man in the doorway matched Pat's tone; an unlit cigar was clamped belligerently in the corner of his mouth.

Dusty recognized the voice at once and she hurried forward. "Dad, I'm sorry. I forgot you were coming over to fix that lamp this morning."

"Dad?" Pat's face softened to a smile. "Many pardons, sir," he said, extending his hand. "I was about to heave your body down the stairs."

"You were about to try," Dusty's father quietly said as he shook Pat's hand. "George Ross, but everybody calls me Dusty."

"Pat Mahoney here," Pat said. "The name Dusty suits you better than it does your daughter."

Her father reached down and picked up his toolbox and brought it into the apartment. "What can you do?" he asked with a shrug. "They steal our names, our sports, and even our underwear."

Pat closed the door and took her father's jacket.

"You don't have to worry about that, sir. Camilla's is still pink and lacy."

Dusty's astonishment was almost enough to keep her speechless. The careful, noncommittal look on her father's face forced an explanation from her. "Pat's my houseman, Dad."

"Oh, is that what they're calling them these days?"

"No, Dad, not that." She laughed nervously. "I pay him. It's his job to take care of me."

"That's good." He carried his toolbox into the living room, stopping before a brass table lamp. "This the one that's broke?"

She nodded, and he spoke before she had a chance. "I'm glad you got somebody staying with you. I never liked the idea of you being alone here." He had the lampshade off and the plug out of the socket before he stopped to grin at Pat. "Been after her for years to get married or at least find herself a live-in boyfriend, so's I could sleep nights."

"Dad, Pat's not my boyfriend. He does the house-keeping and cooking and that kind of stuff."

Her father surveyed Pat from the top of his hand-some head down to his broad feet. "Glad you picked him over Ron," her father said. "Mind you, I have nothing against the guy. He's nice enough, but he's too . . ."

"Intellectual?" Pat suggested.

"Oh, you've met him," Mr. Ross commented.

"Not yet," Pat admitted, and responded to Dusty's glare with an innocent smile before he went back to the kitchen.

By the time her father left after lunch Dusty was able to laugh over the whole misunderstanding, and after a long nap that restored much of her strength she was able to admit that her father was right. It was a good idea to have Pat around. She felt much safer knowing he was in her apartment. That was why his broad shoulders appealed to her and why she liked looking at his muscular arms—because of the security they represented. The doorbell interrupted her thoughts just as the warm flush of that dream was returning.

"It's Jessica, Miss Ross." Her voice came over the intercom, a trifle uncertain and very young. "I brought you some papers from the office that I thought you'd want."

Dusty tried to keep from sounding surprised. Jessica doing something extra? "That's very nice of you, Jessica. Bring them up."

"Can Debbie come up too?"

"Debbie?"

"She's Mr. Millela's secretary. She helped me bring your stuff."

"Certainly."

"And Sue drove us." Jessica went on to explain. "She works in property management."

"Fine. Why don't you all come up?" Dusty quickly buzzed to release the lock and then opened the door and waited at the head of the stairs. If she left them in the lobby any longer, Jessica would be pulling people in off the street.

Jessica came up first, followed by a short blonde and a tall brunette who looked vaguely familiar. Jessica's hands were free, but each of the other two carried a small pile of manila folders.

"This is a surprise," Dusty said. "I wasn't expecting you."

"I talked to your butler," Jessica told her. "He said

to bring the things over anytime after work. He said he'd be here. You know, he doesn't sound like a regular butler."

Dusty took the folders and smiled. "You mean because he has an Irish accent?"

"He sounds sort of young and . . . and husky."

Jessica's voice ended on a breathless sigh and Dusty fought a momentary temptation to send the girls on their way. Instead, she stepped out of the doorway and waved them inside. "Would you like to see the apartment?"

Their immediate agreement could only be called eager. So, putting the folders on the credenza in the foyer, she led them in. They made polite noises about the bay window overlooking the street in the living room, the custom-made bookshelves surrounding the fireplace, and the dining room set. But at the kitchen their interest turned from polite to intense.

"Hello, ladies," boomed a deep, genial voice. Pat turned from the counter to greet them. He had on dark blue slacks and a short-sleeved light-blue shirt that was open at the neck. His short white apron in no way detracted from his masculinity. But with his broad shoulders, deep chest, and narrow waist, not even a lace pinafore could have done that.

"Hi." If was a soft sighing sound that came in unison from the three young female throats. Swell. Just what a Gaelic god needed: a little adulation.

Dusty cleared her throat loudly. "This is Pat Mahoney. He's—he's my butler."

"I'm Jessica. I talked to you this afternoon. Twice."

"I'm Debbie."

"I'm Sue."

Why had she hesitated like that? She was acting like a young kid just out of school. Of course, so were the other three, but they had an excuse. That was exactly what they were.

"Hm, that smells good," Jessica said, sniffing appreciatively. "What are you making?"

"Veal Orloff."

"That sounds delicious," Sue said. "I sure would like the recipe."

Pat laughed easily as a broad smile came to his face. Was he used to females falling all over him? Dusty wondered.

"It really takes more than a recipe. A demonstration would be a lot better."

The three girls looked at one another.

"I'm sure you ladies don't have time for that," Dusty interjected quickly.

"Right," Pat agreed. "Plus my contract with Miss Ross doesn't cover using her home as a school for the culinary arts."

The girls nodded somberly.

"We could use my house," Sue offered, and everyone looked toward her. "Well, my mom's going away for a week. My father and brother would be home, but I could send them out."

Three pairs of eyes turned hopefully toward Pat. Good Lord, Dusty thought. Had she ever been like that?

Pat looked completely relaxed, as if this adulation were the most natural thing in the world, and shrugged his shoulders. "We'll see."

He didn't look exactly in need of rescue, but Dusty provided the service anyway. "We haven't firmed up Pat's free time yet. Plus I have some entertaining to do soon and he will be quite busy."

Their disappointment was very obvious.

Pat shrugged. "She's the boss."

Dusty noticed that whenever he shrugged, his shoulders looked like they wanted to burst out of the seams of his shirt.

"Well," Dusty said brusquely, turning back to the girls. "I really appreciate your taking the time to bring me my work. I certainly don't want to keep you any longer."

"That's okay," Jessica said. "We were planning to go out to dinner in the neighborhood anyway."

"Yeah," Debbie added. "We were glad to do it."

Sue just nodded.

Then Pat broke in. "If you ladies like Greek food, I would recommend the Golden Unicorn. It's three blocks south of here and two over."

The girls looked interested.

"That's close to where we parked," Sue pointed out.

"Would you recommend anything?" Jessica asked Pat.

"Just ask for Gus," Pat said. "Tell him I sent you and he'll take good care of you."

The girls' faces lit up as if they had been given a magnificent gift. They moved eagerly down the hall, and Pat went with them as far as the door. When they had left he smiled and said, "Nice kids."

"Yes, they are," Dusty said absently. The slightest movement on his part caused ripples in muscles throughout his body. Like now, when he quickly wiped his hands on the apron, it caused a ripple to start in his forearm and finish up in his chest.

A puzzled look came to Pat's face, and he glanced down at himself, then up at Dusty. "Does this informal garb offend you?" he asked, indicating his shirt and slacks. "I thought with just the two of us here, I could dress more informally."

Dusty shook herself out of her trance with a start. "Of course you can. Why do you ask?"

"You were staring at me. I thought you didn't like what I was wearing."

"I was not staring at you," she insisted. "I have a lot of things on my mind."

"Oh."

"Now, if you'll excuse me, Mr. Mahoney. I've been away from my office all day and I have a lot of work to catch up on."

"Very good, madam. Is dinner in an hour satisfactory?"

"Quite satisfactory, thank you."

She went into the living room, pulling the papers from one of the folders as she walked, then frowned down at the things in her hand. Why in the world had Jessica thought these were so important that they had to be seen tonight rather than tomorrow? She quickly glanced through the other folders. They were the same, filled with important, but definitely not urgent, material.

Dusty's frown deepened. What had Jessica been thinking of? The muffled sound of the oven door being closed answered the question for her.

Three

Dusty unlocked the door and entered the apartment humming. She felt a little tired, but otherwise fine. Great even, considering it was a Friday evening. Rest and Pat's cooking had recharged her batteries to a new high.

She checked quickly through the neatly sorted mail but found nothing significant and dropped it back down on the credenza. After hanging her raincoat in the hall closet, she walked into the living room. The stillness of the apartment seemed suddenly to press on her, and a cold vise surrounded her chest, clamping off her breath. Where was Pat? He shopped mornings and Tuesday was his day off. He should be here.

"Pat?" Her fearful little query seemed to bounce off the walls and back at her.

"Yo, I'm in my rooms."

Dusty let a sigh of relief escape her as she walked

toward his rooms beyond the kitchen. It was nice to have him around when she got home. She frowned for a moment and corrected herself. It was nice to have *someone* around when she got home. It didn't have to be Pat; it just happened to be him.

The door to his rooms was slightly ajar and she tapped on it. "Are you decent?"

"Always."

"I mean, can I come in?"

"You can go anywhere you want. You own the whole building, remember?"

"Pat, stop fooling around," she said sharply. "Are you dressed to receive guests?"

His shaggy brown hair peeked around the door. There were beads of water on his forehead and his hair was wet. "It depends on the guests. You, I would receive anytime."

Dusty clenched her jaw. "I am just asking how much of your naked body I'll see if I go in there."

"How much do you want to see?"

Why hadn't she just gotten a guard dog like some of her neighbors had?

Pat stepped from behind the door. "Is this enough?"

He had on a pair of jogging shorts, but nothing else. Dusty fought to keep from staring at him. Pat's glistening body looked magnificent.

"Not enough?" His hands went to his waist.

She found her voice. "Enough. Were you taking a shower?"

"I was working out." He waved his arm for her to come in and he picked up a large bath towel from a chair. "What can I do for you?" As he wiped himself off with the towel his muscles rippled.

Dusty forced her gaze away from him. Pat might be

the first butler she'd ever had, but she was sure that it wasn't proper etiquette to ogle him, even if he was a magnificent physical specimen. She pretended interest, instead, in all the exercise equipment spread around the room, the gleaming surfaces reflecting the glow of Pat's body and the flash of blue from the towel.

"You got your equipment set up quickly," she said.

"Had to. I've had it stored for almost two weeks now. That's a long time to be out of training. I was turning flabby."

She hadn't noticed. Suddenly she found her mouth dry, unable to function. She cleared her throat briskly. "Actually I came in to talk about tonight's dinner."

"Okay. Let me get something on and then we can talk."

She nodded as he went into the other room. While he was gone she noted the variety of weights and equipment. Apparently even a Gaelic god had to work to stay in shape.

He was back quickly, with different shorts and a sweatshirt on. His feet were bare. The shirt covered his arms, but her gaze was drawn instead to his long legs. The muscles were delineated as if they had been chiseled from stone. No, stone wasn't right. It wouldn't ripple like that.

"Why don't you sit down?" Pat indicated the one chair in the room while he sat on the weight bench.

"You certainly have a lot of equipment in here," Dusty said.

"I like variety."

In jobs? In women?

"I'm speaking of exercise equipment routines," he clarified.

Was there a leprechaun reading her mind for him? Time to change the subject. "Everything set for tonight's dinner?"

"It'll be perfect. Shrimp remoulade. Cream of spinach soup. Broiled tournedos with sauce bernaise. Italian baked asparagus. And a blitz torte for desert."

"That sounds like a lot to eat."

"Maybe you ought to try out my weights to work up an appetite," he suggested.

"No thanks. Your muscles look good on you, but they wouldn't on me."

"You wouldn't get big muscles."

"I'll pass anyway." She got to her feet and was almost at the door before his voice stopped her.

"Miss Ross?"

She turned.

"How special is this guy Ron?"

Her surprised stare seemed to embarrass him slightly and cause a torrent of words. "I mean, just how should I arrange things for this evening? Soft music? Dim the lights? Do you want me to go to a movie after dinner or stick around in case you two need a referee?"

Was he mocking her? Drawing herself up to her full five feet five inches, she looked down her nose at him. A double measure of frosty dignity was added to her voice. "Ron and I do not indulge in activities that require a referee."

"Ah, right," he said with a nod. "You specialize in intellectual activities."

"Among other things," she added sharply, certain now he was making fun of her. "Which are none of your business."

"I'm just trying to understand what you expect of

me this evening," he told her, his blue eyes as innocent as a babe's.

She wasn't fooled. "I expect a perfect dinner and for
you to melt into the background unless I call you."

"Very good, ma'am." He got to his feet and bowed
slightly, but she didn't wait to see his attempt to melt
into the background. Someone who looked as he did
couldn't melt into the background with all the cam-
ouflage suits the army owned. Ron hadn't been too
enthusiastic when he'd heard she had a butler; she
was afraid to learn his reaction when he saw Pat in
the flesh.

Dusty went into her bathroom and undressed for
her shower. There were all kinds of men in the world,
and different ways of measuring their attractiveness.
So what if Pat was stronger than Ron? All right, taller
too. And better-looking.

Guilt poured in faster than the water from the
shower head. There were other things that were more
important. Like Ron's sensitivity. Pat had been con-
siderate when she was sick and concerned about
pleasing her, but he was being paid to do it.

Dating Ron was a wonderful experience; he was
opening magical doors for her, introducing her to
people she'd never have the chance to meet otherwise. She turned off the water and rubbed herself
briskly with a towel. The chrome fixtures flashed the
wine-colored towel back at her like Pat's equipment
had reflected him and his towel. She gave up trying to
explain her attraction to Ron and, wrapping the towel
around her, went into her bedroom. She didn't need
to justify anything. She and Ron were well suited to
each other. That was all.

When Dusty was finally dressed in a pair of black
pants and a cream-colored satin blouse, her makeup

on and her hair in gentle curls around her shoulders, she frowned into her mirror. She looked good, but was she stunning? She'd rather not let any of Ron's attention wander over to her butler tonight. But as it was ten to seven already, she'd have to be satisfied.

She checked the dining room quickly. Her green place mats and napkins, crystal wineglasses, silver, and fresh flowers were all on the table. Fine, perfect. She rushed into the kitchen. Peace and order reigned there and some of it seeped into her body, pushing her anxiety out.

"Pat."

"Yes, madam," he answered as he turned to face her.

The displaced anxiety came back. Pat had on dark slacks and a white waist-length jacket that covered, but didn't hide, the beautifully sculptured form of his body. Ron would look like a broomstick standing next to Pat.

Guilt rushed in to mix with anxiety and put vinegar in her voice. "Don't you have anything else to wear?"

"This is what I usually wore for formal occasions on the Continent," he said, glancing down at his clothes. "Do you Americans prefer something else?"

"I'm sorry," she stammered embarrassed. "I just wasn't thinking."

He put his arm around her shoulder. "Why don't you go sit down in the living room? Everything is under control here and I promise to behave tonight. Would you like me to get you a little glass of Chablis?"

It felt comfortable in his arms and she nodded.

"Okay, go sit down," he ordered. "I'll bring it in."

Dusty walked in and floated down onto a chair. Her breath seemed to have quickened somewhat. Must be her body making up for the lost time while she was sick, she rationalized.

Pat brought in her glass of wine.

"Madam," he said, bowing slightly with a pleasant smile.

"Thank you, kind sir."

Pat left, but the glow he'd brought stayed with her. She sipped at her wine. She was glad Ron was coming over, that was why she was feeling so good. She had missed him. She took another sip of her wine, catching a faint whiff of the pine-scented cologne Pat used. Ron was the only reason she was feeling good. She finished off the rest of her wine.

Snatches of music drifted into the kitchen where Pat was shredding lettuce. Camilla must have turned on the stereo while waiting for this Ron Samuels fellow, who was—Pat glanced at the clock over the stove—now twenty minutes late. He felt a frown of disapproval crease his forehead. Ah, Mrs. Samuels would be disappointed in her son's poor manners.

A smiling nymph clothed in wonderfully enticing black pants and an ivory blouse floated into his consciousness. Pat shook his head and with a fierce glare sent the nymph scampering back into the living room, where she belonged. Satisfied, he checked the marinating shrimp. What Miss Ross did and whom she saw were none of his concern. He was her butler, paid to serve. He transferred the shrimp to a strainer.

This job was perfect for him. Easy, flexible hours that gave him plenty of time to work with his partners on their planned specialty-shop village and an employer who was undemanding. He had been a little out of line this afternoon with his teasing; the sexual overtones of his remarks had surprised even him, but he'd be more careful in the future. The line between servant and served was for the protection of both. Members of his family had stood on either side of that line and knew it well.

He was glad this Ron was coming over tonight. Patrick Mahoney would show them what a perfect butler he was, unobtrusive but always ready to serve.

He'd treat Camilla the same as he would any other employer. Although it was obvious that unlike his previous employers in Europe she had never had servants before. So she would need a little extra help. As a full-service, flexible butler, he would adjust his services to the needs of the situation.

The doorbell rang and Pat wiped his hands on a towel before hurrying along the hallway to let the great intellectual in. Quickly pushing the thought from his mind, he adjusted his face into a passive, impersonal mask. His job was not to judge, but to serve. Camilla could invite an army of toads over and his courtesy wouldn't falter.

With formal dignity Pat opened the door and ushered Camilla's date in. He allowed himself no more than a passing glance at the man's narrow shoulders, his pale, almost colorless eyes, and the crooked edge of a handkerchief showing in his breast pocket. He concentrated instead on gently pulling the coat from Mr. Samuels' limp arms.

Camilla reached up and kissed Ron on the lips. "I was starting to worry about you," she said. "You were never this late before."

Ron returned the form but not the substance of the kiss. "I was waiting for a parking place to open up close to your building. There were some punks standing around on the corner and I had no intention of running their gauntlet."

Before resolving to be the perfect, nonjudgmental butler, Pat would have thought that a gauntlet of old ladies saying the rosary might be more Mr. Samuels's style, but as it was, the idea barely entered his mind.

"This is Pat Mahoney, Ron. My houseman and butler," Camilla said, but Ron just curtly nodded before walking on into the living room.

"I was lucky a spot opened up finally just down the block. I don't know, Dusty, this neighborhood seems to be getting worse instead of better."

Pat tried not to cringe at the use of the crude nickname. Camilla fit her so much better. It sounded like a flower—soft, delicate, and fragrant. But, of course, it didn't matter to him what her friends called her any more than his opinion of the rapid deterioration of the neighborhood in the last fifteen minutes mattered.

The evening progressed with all the speed and excitement—if Pat had been inclined to notice—of a paralyzed turtle. From the conversation he gathered that Ron was a lawyer with connections. The man dropped so many names that Pat had to step about with care so as not to trip over one.

Sadness and pity eased their way into Pat's heart. He'd seen the care Camilla took to get ready, the excitement in her eyes when he brought her that glass of wine. But instead of tender looks and words of love, she had talk of business and politics. Instead of a hand reaching across to touch hers, she had her napkin to hold. The air should be crackling with the tension of love and desire; instead, it hung heavy with clouds of dullness.

Pat silently removed the soup bowls and was

rewarded with a smile from Camilla. He returned it, seasoned with a wink, as he served her salad.

It really wasn't his place to keep the spirit of joy at the party, but Mahoneys never shrank from uncommon tasks. His father had always said, if you took the king's shilling, you buried your own opinions and went forward with the task at hand. Not that it was really a task to smile at Camilla.

He noted with approval that she attacked the main course with gusto while Ron approached the dish with the listlessness of someone who had given up the spirit, if not the essence of life. He poked and speared with his fork as if he needed to kill the beef first. Pat gave him until long after Camilla was finished and then removed the plates before bringing in the dessert. Camilla's eyes lit up and she murmured a "looks good." Ron stared and then blinked his eyes once like a lethargic carp.

Camilla's zest for attack continued. Ron didn't trust his skills and tried to kill the torte first. Sighing, Pat busied himself about the kitchen for a few minutes before he returned.

"May I take your plate, madam?"

She had finished her meal beautifully. Soup, salad, entree, vegetable, dessert. It was clean plates all evening for Camilla. His mother would have loved the little lass.

"Yes, thank you," she replied. "It was all just absolutely delicious."

"Thank you, madam. Would you like an after-dinner drink? Drambuie perhaps?"

"Why not?" she said brightly.

"And you, sir?"

The man shook his head.

Pat cleared his plate. The dessert had barely been touched. "You did not like the torte, sir?"

"I have a tennis match tomorrow," Ron said. "I don't want to be too sluggish."

"That match isn't until eleven," Camilla pointed out.

"That kind of stuff sticks," Ron insisted. "You'd better be careful. You keep eating all these rich sauces and desserts and you'll blossom out like a blimp."

"Pat is going to develop an exercise program for me to stay in shape," she said, laughing and giving a wink to Pat.

"I forgot," Ron said. "The full-service butler."

"He meets my needs," Camilla replied as she drained her wineglass.

"I'll bring your drink into the living room, madam."

Dusty stared down at the street. Ron's car had long since pulled away, but she was not gazing fondly in the direction it had gone, just staring blankly at the streetlight. Their evening had been lacking somehow, but she couldn't exactly say why.

"Mr. Samuels leave, ma'am?"

"Yes." She turned only after the words had hung in the air a moment, then she moved slowly away from the window. Her eyes slid over the sofa—no echoes of passion lingering there in the neatly fluffed pillows— and onto the end table, with its two empty glasses. Hesitantly her gaze found Pat's chest—his jacket and tie were gone and his shirt collar had been opened— then darted up to his eyes. The mockery she'd feared would be hiding there was absent, but so was the warmth. He was the formal, precise butler he'd been all evening. Just what he was paid to be, so why did she find that disappointing?

"I trust that everything was satisfactory." He picked up the glasses and wiped a ring from the table.

"Yes, it was fine. The meal was delicious."

"Will there be anything else, madam?"

She shook her head and watched as he started down the hall. She wasn't too sleepy, but she guessed she'd go to bed. Or she could read for a while. Though she would really rather have some company.

"Pat." Her voice stopped him at the kitchen door. Why not? He was her employee, after all. "Is there any more of that blitz torte? I'm in the mood for a midnight snack, even if it's only eleven."

"Very good, madam."

She followed him into the kitchen. His broad back was turned toward her as he worked with neat, crisp movements. He was so big, so masculine that he ought to look strange in the kitchen, yet he didn't. How, if Ron were there, unwrapping the blitz torte . . .

The picture brought a smile to her face, but it faded quickly. Ron. Maybe that was what had happened to the teasing Pat of that afternoon.

She sat down at the kitchen table, kicking off her shoes and tucking her feet under her. The words seemed awkward to force out, making her voice loud in the small kitchen. "I'm sorry about the way Ron acted. He's really very nice. . . ." She let her voice die away, not knowing what to say to excuse his rudeness to Pat.

"I beg your pardon?" A knife poised above the torte, Pat was frozen into total bewilderment. "Why are you apologizing to me for him?"

The weave of the tablecloth captured her gaze,

though her tongue was still free to falter. "Well, he was so rude, not saying anything when I introduced you and—" Pat's laughter released her eyes.

"Most people don't introduce their servants to their guests," he pointed out. "Mr. Samuels knows our place in the world."

Irritation stiffened her spine and washed away the embarrassment. "Just because you work for me that doesn't make you less a person."

"I know." The blue eyes danced above his broad smile. Damn. He was laughing at her, she realized. "Then why shouldn't I introduce you to my guests?" she asked hotly.

He put her piece of torte down before her. "If you don't know, perhaps you should ask Mr. Samuels."

A condescending answer if she'd ever heard one. She stuck a forkful of the pastry into her mouth, its creamy strawberry goodness sweetening her annoyance into devilment as she watched Pat wrap up the remaining torte.

"Why don't you join me?" she asked.

She couldn't decide if his eyes were mocking her again when he replied. "Is that an order from a lady to her servant?"

"Yes." Her eyes mocked back, but would not let him go. Blindly she put another forkful of the torte into her mouth and smiled with satisfaction. "I won't force the calories on you, but you shall keep me company." She nodded toward the chair next to her.

"I'm sure Mr. Samuels wouldn't approve." He cut himself a piece of torte and sat down. "But a servant's job is to obey." The words were said simply, but his half-smile teased her. Dusty looked down momentarily to regroup.

His chair was around the corner of the table, not

that close, but suddenly not very far either. He had rolled up his shirt-sleeves and exposed to Dusty's view all the dark hairs on his thick arm. Strong and rough, like his voice, yet those hands were capable of delicate work like making this gorgeous dessert. If she moved just slightly, their arms would brush. Would his skin be warm like his eyes or cool like his laugh?

She moved, but in the opposite direction, concentrating on spearing a large strawberry. She popped it into her mouth. "So how'd you ever become a butler? Was it something you always wanted to be?"

He smiled. "Actually I was counting on fortune and fame, and it seemed a close second."

"Come on."

"Oh, so it's my life history you'll be wanting, is it?" He slipped into a thick Irish broque. "And slave that I am, I must obey."

"Right." She finished the last of her torte and pushed the plate into the center of the table. "What part of Ireland are you from?"

"The part that's rich in beauty."

Was there laughter or pain, humor or mockery in his expression? She couldn't really tell. Maybe a little of each.

"Plenty of food to sustain the soul, but almost none for the boy." He finished his torte and picked up both dishes. "Want me to make some coffee? Or maybe a brandy would help you sleep better."

"I'll have one if you'll join me."

His eyes gave her no clue to the thoughts dancing in his head, but he got two snifters out of the cabinet. "Actually I don't remember living in Ireland at all. We moved to Liverpool when I was just a lad. My father got a job on the docks, my mother worked in a factory between having babies, then she took in sewing."

He poured the dark liquor into the glasses and carried them over to her. "I'd always loved sports better than academics, so when a football club—soccer club to you Americans—offered me a contract to play on their junior team, I accepted and left home to live and train with them."

"How old were you?"

"Fourteen."

"Gracious." She sipped her brandy and thought back. "When I was fourteen the only job I could get was baby-sitting the Stasiak twins."

"There were tradeoffs though. I thought I was done with school until they told me I needed to learn a trade besides kicking a soccer ball. My grades, at the time, were pointing away from serious studying, so they gave me the choice of chef or plumber. Since food was on my mind whenever it wasn't in my mouth, I went to cooking school and apprenticed with local chefs in the off-season. I kept on learning and working after I was traded to Manchester United and a few years later to a French team, then an Austrian club, a Spanish one, and finally to an American team."

"What about your home?" she asked. "Do you ever get back there?"

"To Liverpool?" He shook his head and downed the last of his brandy. "No, my parents are both dead and my brothers scattered. Besides, I learned long ago that home is where I hang my hat."

"I envy all the traveling you've done.

"I'm lucky to have had the chance," He was quiet for a long moment. "Unfortunately my sons probably won't be able to drink of the same variety. Progress is swallowing all the individualists of the world and spitting out carbon copies."

"You have a wife and family, then?" Hardly reason for the wave of loneliness washing over her.

"No." His eyes laughed at her even though his lips were still. "I was speaking of the future, supposing somewhere in the world there is a lass who'll have me."

A lass? There would be hundreds, thousands probably, who'd have him based on his looks alone if they knew he was on the market. Add his gentle, caring ways and she'd have to beat them away with a stick.

She? Why was she assuming she'd want to keep the other women away from him? He was her butler, that was all. Not someone she was involved with. Not someone she'd be jealously protecting. She got to her feet, feeling tired, the weariness of the week finally catching up with her.

"I think I'll turn in," she said. "Thanks for the snack."

He got up and went to the dishwasher. "I'll get the lights in the living room. I like to check out the house before I turn in," he called over his shoulder.

Already they had fallen into a routine: safe, compatible, schedules, like her and Ron. She ought to be pleased.

Four

The Industrial Revolution, the American revolution, the French revolution. Dusty slammed the history book shut, starting her own little Ross revolution. Her night school advisor had reminded her of the need to take something other than business courses if she wanted a degree, but Dusty had failed to realize how hard it would be to study with gorgeous spring Saturdays and a hunk of a butler to distract her. If studying under those conditions wasn't a sin, it was surely against the law.

"Finished with your studying, ma'am?" Pat was replacing the last of her books on the shelves after dusting them.

"Sort of." She'd been watching him work for the past half-hour, while pretending to study. Why play games? She pushed her textbook from her line of sight and smiled.

"I've been thinking about that exercise program

you offered to plan for me. Would any of it entail outside activities?"

Pat's eyes only darted briefly toward the sunshine
spilling in through the front window. "Bicycling is
excellent exercise. And there are shops that rent
them over in Lincoln Park."

"I'd hate to pull you away from your schedule, but I
really feel the need to begin the program immediately."

His eyes remained almost serious. "I'm yours to command, madam. Just let me change into something
more suitable."

Dusty's eyes followed him out of the room and
down the hall, her mind refusing to allow her neck to
strain and stretch to keep him in sight a few extra
seconds. She got to her feet and sedately walked
down to her room. She was not some sex-starved
teenager reduced to ogling her butler. He had been
living here with her for more than a week now, and
she was used to seeing him. He had no more effect on
her than the mailman. She closed her door with a
frown, not wanting to pursue that issue at all.

In fifteen minutes, dressed in jeans and light jack-
ets, she and Pat left the house and headed east
toward Lincoln Park and Lake Michigan. The temperature was only in the fifties, but there was a pleasant
warmth glowing inside her that matched the sunshine in the air. She took a deep breath and smiled at
the solid giant next to her.

"How come a macho man like you isn't into
jogging?" she asked.

"Can't," he answered. "These ankles have carried
me in too many soccer games. They've retired." As if
in answer to her quizzical look, he went on. "The
right ankle's been broken twice and I've broken bones
in the left foot three times."

"Why did you keep on playing?"

"It's part of the game," he said, shrugging. "Everything in this world has a price."

She thought of the history assignment she'd abandoned for this morning in the sunshine. "Was the price worth it?"

"I've gotten more than I'd ever hoped for as a lad," he said. "I've traveled to every continent except Antarctica. I've shaken the hands of presidents, African tribal chiefs, desert sheikhs, and Calcutta beggars. Memories to last me forever. That's not too bad for a poor boy from Liverpool."

Dusty continued watching the sidewalk as they strolled side by side, but she could feel their spirits reaching out and holding hands. His leaving Liverpool was like her flight from the southside Canaryville neighborhood where she'd been raised. They were kindred spirits running from the shackles of their past. Or were they? He was content to survive on memories while living at the beck and call of someone else. She was always fighting to be her own master.

The warm spring air blew such depressing thoughts from her mind, and by the time they reached the bicycle shop she didn't care about anything. She was too glad that the sun was shining and the breeze was gently warm. She felt alive and happy, and Pat's laughter at the skip in her step only increased those feelings.

The shop was crowded with other couples wanting to welcome spring along the bike paths in the park, and Dusty felt sudden confusion. They weren't a couple; they were employer and employee. Should she offer to pay for the bicycles? Why wasn't she here with Ron, on a date like all these other young women? Not that she really wanted that. Days bursting with springtime and newness weren't exactly Ron's thing. Did it really matter that she was paying Pat a salary? She could enjoy the day with him anyway.

It was their turn, and Pat ordered the bikes before Dusty's mouth was even half open, making her feel like a fool. Pat has handled these situations before. He'd pay and she'd reimburse him later. She was seeing problems where none existed. Their relationship was not as complicated or embarrassing as she seemed to think.

Taking their bikes, they chose a route winding north through Lincoln Park, along the narrow paved paths, past strollers and joggers and kite flyers. The wind was ruffling her hair, pulling it free of the ponytail and dancing it around her face. Everything smelled wet and new. The tires made smacking noises as they hit puddles, then pulled a trail of water out after them. She felt wonderful—free and happy and alive.

Pat was riding a little ahead and her eyes found the sight of him to their liking. His blue nylon windbreaker was stretched tightly over his shoulders, and his worn jeans caressed his lower body with love. A rivet on the corner of one of his back pockets caught the sun and winked at her.

Pat was part of the springtime, coming into her life at the same time as the warm sun. His laugh was the spring breeze, warming her soul to life. His eyes were the gentle rains that made everything feel new. She grinned with pure happiness and, pulling around on the grass, raced ahead of him.

"Oh-ho, so we're getting lively, are we?" His voice carried his laughter like the breezes carry the sun.

She raced along the clear stretch of path, feeling

him close behind. His presence reached out to her like fingers straining to touch, a hold she wanted and didn't want. Pedaling faster, she stayed ahead. The front wheel of his bike was visible from the corner of her eye, but she didn't need to see it to know he was there. A delicious tension was creeping up her spine, curling her toes and making her blood race.

She sped up a slight incline, her legs working harder than they wanted, harder than they were used to, but she was too caught up in the race to slow down. She had to beat him to the street ahead. Why, she didn't know. It was part of the day, part of the magic in the sunshine. She wanted to run and laugh and feel like a child again, yet at the same time there was an awareness that she was very much a woman.

From out of a side path hidden by bushes two joggers appeared, coming right toward her. After a moment of confused back-pedaling Dusty squeezed her handbrakes. The bike skidded to a stop, balancing upright for a second, then wobbling precariously.

"Steady there." Pat laughed and reached out to catch her.

The touch of his arm around her shoulders produced a warmth no butler ought to be able to cause. Her breath seemed to desert her, and she leaned into him, gulping in air, trying to slow her pounding heart.

"I think I won," she said. Only after her laugh echoed through her body and returned her sanity was she brave enough to turn slightly to look at him. His laughing eyes seemed to engulf her; his mouth was warm and near and calling to her.

"I don't remember a race being called," he teased. "Madam wouldn't be trying to cheat, would she?"

"Never," she cried, grateful for his reminder of reality.

She pulled away from him gently, not as if his touch had become painful, but as if she were ready to ride again. And she was. Her head clear, her senses restored, her vision unfettered. Pat was her butler, her employee. She was not as snobbish about these things as Ron, but there was one issue she had to face. She paid his salary. He was nice to her because he was paid to be nice. He was paid to smile, to laugh, to go bike-riding with her. In her enjoyment of his company she had better not lose sight of that fact.

She climbed back onto her bike. "Shall we ride through the zoo or around it?"

"Whatever you want."

Of course, how could she keep forgetting? "Let's go around it, then. My navigational skills aren't quite up to par yet."

The paths on the east side of the park, away from the small, city-run zoo, were less crowded, and she and Pat could ride side by side. They spoke little, just enjoying the day and the exercise.

At the north end of the park they turned farther east, crossing under Lake Shore Drive to Lake Michigan itself. There were fewer people here, and the wind off the lake had more chill to it. They got off their bikes to sit on the sand in companionable silence as they watched the whitecaps racing toward the shore.

Pat rose first. "Come on," he said. "If you sit around too much, your muscles will stiffen up."

Dusty took his hand and pulled herself up. "'Fraid it's too late."

"It hasn't been that long," he protested. "Get back on the bike."

"Slave driver," she shouted at the broad back already riding away.

Instead of going back through the park, they rode along the concrete walkway that edged the beach. The air was crisper here, the wind coming straight in off the lake without any trees to deflect its strength, but it felt good. To stay warm she had to keep pedaling, but it didn't seem a chore.

Ahead of them were the high-rise apartments of the Gold Coast, honeycombs of the wealthy and famous. "Aren't they gorgeous?" she said to Pat, nodding toward the buildings.

He shrugged. "Some of the older buildings are interesting," he admitted. "But I like your neighborhood better."

"You're kidding! Gang mottoes spray-painted on walls, boarded-up windows, and garbage in the alleys! Have you really taken a good look around you?"

"It's got character."

"But it's all dilapidated!"

They crossed over to the southern end of the park and made their way back to the bike shop. As she'd guessed, Pat paid for the bicycles, but she took the receipt from the attendant and tucked it into her pocket.

"Now what, coach?" she asked.

He took her arm, but she was able to ignore the fact that it awakened feelings far different from those Ron stirred up. Did he even stir up any? The most she remembered feeling with him lately was tired.

"A leisurely walk home to a light, healthful lunch," Pat said.

Rather than heading back straight west, they went north a few blocks, walking past the trendy shops and restaurants of the chic Lincoln Park area. Dusty took a careful interest in the windows they were passing, certainly not because she wanted to distract her thoughts from the man next to her, she told herself, but because the stores were so amusing.

The pet store offered genuine fur coats for dogs and its own blend of cat food. A hamster in the window had an intricate system of tunnels and rooms to climb through, more square-foot space per pound of inhabitant than she had in her apartment. A children's clothing store offered genuine American Indian costumes—Sioux, Apache, or Navajo. And the health food store had bean curd on sale.

"Let's turn here," Pat said.

"How do you know this neighborhood so well?" Dusty wondered suddenly. "You've lived here for such a short time."

"I've actually been around a little over a year," Pat said. "Besides, I was in and out a lot when my American teams came in to play the Chicago Sting."

"What did you do before I hired you?" she asked.

"Oh, this and that," he said, not wanting to talk about the months he'd spent organizing investors for his project, scouting locations, and talking to bankers. Then a broad smile broke across his face. "But I started running low on cash and decided an old man like me needed a steady job."

"You're not that old."

"Maybe not in years," he said, the smile softening somewhat. "But I certainly am in miles traveled. We international athletes live a fast life."

"I see," she murmured.

But she didn't really. Dusty could never understand lack of ambition. How could he just let himself drift, blown about by the fates like a fluff of dandelion seed blown about by the winds? Here today, gone tomorrow.

They walked on in silence. There were fewer and fewer store windows to stare into, and Dusty was forced either to acknowledge her thoughts or start chattering. She found Pat attractive. He was companionable and witty, fun to be around. But personal involvement was out. She was too busy for that anyway, what with work and night school and Ron. Lord, if she were looking for involvement, she ought to start with Ron, not with a Gypsy likely to be gone with the next full moon.

They turned a corner, and Dusty looked around her. "You can't really mean that you like this better than the Gold Coast."

"Sure." He pointed to an old brownstone across the street. "Look at the stonework in that building. It was made with pride and craft, not with a mold."

She shrugged, noticing for the first time the graceful symmetry under the years of dirt and soot. "But you can't walk down the street without worrying about being mugged."

"That'll change. When there are enough people here who love the area, it'll be safe." He took her arm and nodded toward a shoe repair shop they were passing. "The owner of this shop learned his trade from his father in Europe years and years ago. Did you know that he can custom-make shoes, beautiful ones, and charges less than the two hundred dollars men would pay Florsheim's for the same shoe? Yet people ask him only to put on a new set of heels."

An old man in the window of the store looked up. His wrinkled face creased into a smile and he waved. Pat waved back and Dusty weakly echoed his movements.

"And there's an old woman, a few blocks over, who gives piano lessons," Pat went on. "She once played with the Austrian Symphony, but she's almost blind and there aren't too many kids in the neighborhood, so her lessons are few and far between. How can you say this place doesn't have character?"

She looked around her uneasily, as if the neighborhood she thought she knew was turning against her. It had been hiding things. "I'll be better once renovation comes," she said. "Safer."

He shook his head. "Tomas's rent will be raised so high that he can't pay it, and Mrs. Hildenburg will be pressured to sell since she can't afford renovation."

"I doubt that they're happy with the gangs," Dusty pointed out.

"No." Pat's voice weakened. "But there ought to be a middle ground."

"I'll just be happy when I'm not worrying about more burglaries."

His brogue reappeared with his smile. "What? You're still trembling with fear, and big, strong Paddy at your side? Ach, he must be losing his touch." His teasing kept up until they got home.

"I don't think it's right of Camilla to leave you home all alone," Dusty Senior announced, and took another drink of his beer.

Pat's smile was hidden as he stirred the pot of chili he was making. "That's part of my job." Waiting and welcoming Camilla home wasn't a chore, though he wished she were spending her time with someone a bit more worthy. Seeing more of Mr. Samuels had not bettered his image in Pat's mind and it was getting harder not to point out his many failings to Camilla.

Pat tasted a bit of the chili, and added more chili powder, then came back to the table and his own beer. Camilla's father had dropped by after she and Ron had already left for a party, but had accepted Pat's invitation to join him for dinner.

"I'm her butler, not her boyfriend," Pat reminded him.

"That's another thing I don't understand." Mr. Ross took the unlit cigar from his mouth and jabbed it in the air. "Now, I know you're younger than me, and your bulk is muscle while mine is flab, but I gotta ask you anyway, even if you decide to beat the hell out of me." He paused for a gulp of beer. "What the hell is a big, strong guy like you doing in a kitchen?"

Pat didn't take offense. "Most of the world's great chefs are men."

Dusty Senior waved the words away with his cigar. "I'm talking about you. I saw you play with the Tea Men years ago and with the Sockers. You could get a real job if you tried."

"This is a real job. I like it and I'm good at it."

"But is it what you want to do forever?"

Forevers weren't in his future, not just yet. He got to his feet, ready to set the table, with knives, forks, and spoons in one hand, bowls in the other. Being a butler suited him right now. It gave him a place to live without draining the capital he needed for his investment. And it gave him plenty of free time during the day to pursue his project.

Of course, this particular job seemed to come with some unusual problems. He'd gotten expert at avoiding entanglements, at making sacrifices in the present so his dreams could have reality in the future. But lately the dreams had been nudging harder at him. A vague wispy figure was invading his nights, laughing with Camilla's laugh as she teased him to find someone to hold. Someone to be a part of, to plan and hope with. Someone to love so fiercely that life itself was nothing without her. He would have all that soon, with a little luck, but letting the fates hear his hopes was not smart.

"It's what I'm trained for," he finally said.

Mr. Ross seemed content to drop the subject. He finished his beer and leaned back. "I went to have my shoe fixed this afternoon. Tore the heel right off yesterday."

Pat did not think sympathy or remorse was expected. He just got another beer out of the refrigerator, opened it, and put it down before Camilla's father.

"Tomas told me a strange story about my daughter's butler. Seems he's got some big real estate deal in the works."

Pat's frown twisted more inside him than on the outside. Should he risk being discourteous, or hope the fates were sleeping? "Hardly big," he said lightly. He put the pot of chili in the middle of the table. "It's just a project I've been trying to get off the ground for a while now."

"It a secret?"

"Not really." Pat ladled chili into the bowls. "Me and a few friends are trying to put together a shopping center here in the city. One third restaurants and the rest stores. Small, high-quality specialty-type stores with some real, old world craftsmen. We've got a number of merchants lined up, but we're having a hard time finding the right location at the right price."

"You talked to Camilla about it? She could probably help."

That shadowy figure from his dreams danced

through his mind. Her eyes were blue—deep, dark and cool. Mountain lakes whose depths held secrets hidden. "It wouldn't be right to ask."

Mr. Ross shrugged. "That's her job. She finds you something good, she earns a commission. What kind of a problem is that?"

"I don't want to impose myself on her," Pat insisted. It was a matter of principle. A man took care of his own; he didn't take from them.

Dusty leaned back in the seat and tried to stay awake. Ron had been at her side during the party, but not because he was interested in talking to her. She had felt like a decorative appendage as he wheeled and dealed with the other guests. She hadn't been in the mood for making business contacts, so wine had been her companion. And the first glass had brought relatives, too many of them.

Forcing her eyes to stay open, Dusty gingerly stretched one leg, then the other one, in the dark confines of Ron's BMW. She was starting to stiffen up from her bicycle ride that morning. Her eyes slipped closed again. Maybe Pat would know some remedies for aching muscles.

"This has been an outstanding evening."

She forced her eyes open, struggling against the vision of Pat's hands soothing away her soreness, and looked over at Ron. He was staring straight ahead down the street, so she gratefully closed her eyes again, sensing his excitement from the tone of his voice and the way his hands gripped the steering wheel.

"A pleasurable evening with the right people," he

went on. "And it has the potential to be highly profitable."

She murmured an agreement.

The silence that followed grew uncomfortably long, and Dusty could feel Ron's eyes scolding her. She ignored him, pulling the vision of Pat's hands back toward her. It wouldn't come.

"I'd think that you'd be more thrilled than I," he said. "From a personal and a professional point of view."

The headache that had been on the edge of her consciousness all evening now decided to arrive, and the chill in her feet started to creep upward. As usual, Ron's perfect parking place had turned out to be several blocks from the party. An overcast sky had fulfilled its promise with a downpour just as they were leaving. Somehow her feet seemed to have gotten the worst of things and were now cold and wet. She tried to ignore her various discomforts and go back to dreaming of those hands.

"The contacts you made tonight could do wonders for your career," Ron said. "You should have paid closer attention to them."

"I laughed at their jokes, nodded at their wisdom, and looked fascinated even when I was bored. What more should I have done, kiss their feet?"

"I didn't realize it was such an effort for you."

Dusty was too tired to argue anymore. Her eyes closed again and she repeated, over and over again, that her feet were not cold. If only those hands could come back, she'd be warm again. If only Ron would stop talking.

What was wrong with her? Her eyes flew open, her feet forgotten as she stared out into the rainy night. A few weeks ago she would have rushed to please Ron, changing her opinions to match his. Last week she would have at least pretended to agree with him. This week she just didn't care anymore. It wasn't a matter of being too tired.

Turning her head, she watched the rain-washed streets go by. The only recent change in her life was Pat. She was losing interest in Ron because of Pat, and that was the riskiest of propositions. Better for her to come down with the flu again.

"Do you want me to let you off at the corner or in front of your building?" Ron asked.

"It doesn't matter." She tried, and failed, to convince herself that Pat's smile had nothing to do with her sudden dissatisfaction. "Whatever's convenient for you."

"I'll let you off in front of your door," he said. "Traffic's light, so I can double-park for a minute."

He splashed to a stop in front of her building, put the car in neutral, and set the emergency brake. Releasing himself from his seat belt, he leaned over to kiss her on the cheek.

"I'll call you Monday at eight," he said, and refastened his seat belt.

It was just as always. He called Mondays at eight; they had drinks Wednesdays after work; dinner was on Fridays. No surprises, no passion, no fun. "No more."

"Huh?"

She surprised herself as well as Ron by saying the words out loud, but once she had started, everything seemed to come out. "As a business relationship we're fine, but as lovers we've got nothing."

"I beg your pardon?"

He sounded so wounded that she almost felt sorry for him, except that she was suddenly so depressed herself. "There's no magic. No spark. No wild excitement."

"I didn't realize that was what you were looking for."

"No?" That said something in itself. She opened the door. "So long, Ron. Thanks for everything."

She stepped out into the street, the pouring rain adding to the depression washing over her. It wasn't that she cared about Ron. It was just that she was twenty-nine and still as alone as she had been at twenty. All she had to show for her time was her career, and that didn't make her laugh or keep her warm at night.

A husky figure with an umbrella met her as she squeezed between two parked cars. "You didn't have to wait up," she told Pat.

"You didn't take your umbrella like I told you." He put his arm around her shoulder to pull her closer into his shelter. Why should her butler's arm feel more protective than Ron's had? Could she only get comfort by paying for it? The BMW roared off behind them, the exhaust of her useless relationship swirling around her.

"This is a cold, chilling rain." Pat's scolding continued as he hurried her up the narrow sidewalk to the door. "You'll be sick again at this rate."

She was already sick. Sick of being alone. Sick of looking for Prince Charming. She didn't mind finding out that her hero had feet of clay, but did the rest of him have to match. Couldn't she find someone with a little heart, a little love to give? She trudged up the stairs ahead of Pat.

"Your feet are all wet. What were you doing, playing out in the rain?" Pat opened the apartment door and hurried her inside, misreading her sad smile. "It's nothing to laugh about," he continued, his thick black eyebrows frowning at her along with his lips. "You're going to be back in bed before you know it."

"Is that a threat or a promise?"

Her words echoed in the air, the gentle, sad joke suddenly serious. Was she destined always to be alone, with only her pillow to cuddle through the night? The promise of love, of warmth and passion, always fleeing from her?

Her eyes locked with Pat's. Surprise at her question was on his face, but that was all she could read. Or was it shock? Did he think she was propositioning him? Was she? Warmth crept up over her face, molten lava igniting her senses. His lips, his eyes, his gentle breath, awoke hungers in her, even as the searing heat froze her lips and vocal cords in embarrassment.

"You'd better get out of those wet clothes." Pat looked away first; was it strength or lack of interest? His voice was soft as he helped slide her coat off her arms. "I'll put this in the laundry room to dry. Get the rest of your clothes off and I'll take care of them."

She strove to bring the soft detachment of his voice into her own thoughts. Her mind was leading her in dance steps she was unfamiliar with, leaving her confused and dizzy. So Ron wasn't her one and only; she'd had disappointments in love before, more than once. That didn't mean there was no hope. She'd find someone one day. Someone who'd love her back.

"Everything else is pretty dry," she said, but Pat was already moving down the hall. "Pat—"

She followed him into her bedroom, where he pulled her thick, furry yellow robe and matching slippers from the closet. The robe made her look like a jaundiced bear. Was that how everyone saw her? Unattractive and unappealing?

"I hate that robe," she cried, her voice quivering with sudden tears. "It makes me look ugly."

"Ma'am?"

She grabbed the thing from his hands and sank onto the end of her bed, hugging it and fighting back tears. "I'm a woman, you know. I may not be athletic or Miss America quality, but I'm not all that bad."

She sniffed loudly, inelegantly—Ron would have been shocked—and stared at Pat's feet. His shoes were wet.

"Are you all right, Miss Ross?" Pat's shoes came closer, and the bed moved as he sat down next to her.

She used the robe to wipe the tears from her cheeks, but Pat stole it and put his white handkerchief in its place. "The handkerchief's easier to wash than the robe," he explained gently.

She tried to smile, feeling like the ultimate fool, and found her face muscles unwilling to perform the task. "Always practical, aren't you?" Her eyes were locked on the floor.

"Not always."

His arm went around her shoulders. It was comforting, brotherly. Still, she guessed she had to take what she could get.

"What's wrong?"

She sighed and leaned into his shoulder. She couldn't see him—didn't want to see him—but his strength was there. "I told Ron to jump in the lake."

"That seems like cause for celebration, not tears." His voice was sympathetic, a soft, cleansing rain on the city streets.

"I know. He was a jerk."

"But you cared for him."

"Not really." Why was she spilling her heart out to him? He was a stranger. "It's just—" She couldn't voice her thoughts.

His arm tightened, pulling her closer, telling her she wasn't alone. For the moment she'd ignore the fact he was her employee, that she paid his salary and bought his concern.

"It's just what?"

She laid her head on his shoulder and closed her eyes. She already appeared the idiot, why be embarrassed about adding a little spice to the recipe? "I'm twenty-nine-years old," she blurted out. "I want to be in love. I want someone to love me. I can't keep wasting months and years on selfish jerks who can't even walk me to the door." She gulped back the rush of tears that threatened to steal her voice. "You're the only one who seems to like me, and I pay you to do it."

Pat did not reply, but Dusty could feel an extra dose of protectiveness flow around her. His hand moved in a comforting, circular motion on her back. She melted farther into his arms. Although she knew that it was just the wine relaxing her body, she let herself enjoy it a little.

"You must think I'm stupid," she said with a sigh. "And I guess you're right."

"I think you're one of the nicest and prettiest ladies I know," he said. "And I think you're tired. After a good night's sleep you're going to realize that you're better off without Mr. Samuels."

"It's not him."

His finger came over her lips gently to silence her. "And one of these days someone's going to come along to sweep you off your feet, someone who sees the special lady that I do, and you'll forget any lonely days you might have spent."

She was too tired to move; her tears had drained the strength from her. The nook of his arms was so comfortable. "How did you get so wise, Pat?"

He didn't answer her question, but carefully got to his feet and handed her the soft flannel nightgown he'd taken from the closet. "Get changed and into bed," he said. "I'll make you some tea and you'll feel lots better."

Arguing was beyond her. She nodded and obeyed once he'd left the room. She knew she ought to be embarrassed, especially when she saw her tear-stained, makeup-streaked face in the bathroom mirror, but she just turned away and took a shower. She was tired, dispirited, and unable to think and move at the same time. Pat had said get ready for bed, so that was what she had to do. He was waiting for her when she came out of the bathroom, damp hair clinging to her neck, her feet bare.

"Into bed," he said, and pulled back her covers.

She sat back against the pillows and let him tuck her in, wishing he were staying with her. She'd like to be held. She'd like his arms to keep her safe, his hands to make her warm, and his lips to tell her she was lovable. She'd like to lie in his arms all night.

She fought back the foolish dreams and took the mug of tea from his hands. "I'm sorry I was such an idiot. Maybe I'm still not over the flu."

His eyes took away her embarrassment. "It's probably the grape speaking out and using your lips. You'll feel better tomorrow. Drink the tea quickly." She did so. "Hm-m," he said. "maybe I'll plan a special exercise session."

"Uh-oh."

He smiled and took the empty mug from her hands. "Now, no brooding. Let the angels rock you to sleep."

Was he one of them? "Yes, sir." She slid down in her bed and pulled the covers around her. Already her eyes were drooping and she could feel the warmth of Pat's tea seeping through her, easing her tensions. She imagined a gentle touch on her forehead. A hand most likely, though it was as soft as a kiss. Then the light went out and soft footsteps left the room. He had said she was special. A smile curved her lips and she snuggled farther under the covers.

Five

Dusty slept like a baby, substituting dreams of Pat's arms for the real thing, but morning came all too quickly and with it embarrassment. Dumping Ron caused her no distress, but crying in Pat's arms had not been among her most mature actions. She buried herself in a research paper for history class, vowing to avoid Pat's gaze and him until her crazy fascination with him died.

Keeping clear of Pat was easy to do on Monday by working late, and Tuesday she went to school right after work. But Pat was waiting up for her when she returned home.

"I thought you were going out to celebrate St. Patrick's Day," she said.

"I was too worried about you to enjoy myself," he scolded her. "This is a terrible time for you to be coming home alone."

She dumped her books onto the credenza and

allowed him to help her with her coat. "I've been doing it for five years now."

"Then I shouldn't have to tell you."

She moved her books to the desk in the living room. The house smelled warm and welcoming, like hot soup and fresh bread, and exhaustion sloped her shoulders slightly.

"Working late occasionally is bad enough, but taking classes at this hour twice a week is pure foolishness." He trailed along after her, an angry, possessive Irish chieftain. "What good is all that education going to do you if you're murdered in some dark alley?"

"I don't hang about in dark alleys." She kicked off her shoes and sank her toes into the rug. She bent over to pick up her shoes, only to discover that Pat already had them.

"What is so wonderful about this degree you want that it's worth working yourself sick to get it?"

Since when had he become so protective? She took her shoes from his hand and trudged down the hall to her room.

"Are you going to get a better job?" he asked.

"No." She tossed her shoes into a corner of her bedroom and sank onto her bed.

"Are you going to earn more money?" He picked up the shoes and put them in the closet. She was too tired to feel guilty.

"No." She fell back on the bedspread, her eyes closing. "I'm going to prove I'm as good as all the degreed jerks in the office."

She felt him move closer. "Don't all those sales awards prove that?"

One eye had the strength to open and glare at him. "You have something against a person trying to achieve? Trying to better herself?"

"Not for the right reasons."

His glare was stronger than hers, so her eye gave up.

"Proving something to yourself is fine," he said. "Proving something to others is a waste of time. They rarely care enough to pay attention or to change their minds."

Somewhere deep down under all the exhaustion she suspected he was right, but also suspected it was not exactly as simple as she'd made it out to be. It wasn't just a matter of showing her coworkers; there were those teachers in high school who had favored the college-bound, and the world in general, which measures capability in terms of the college one had attended.

Pat took her hand and pulled her into an upright position. Surprise at his touch opened her eyes.

"Come on," he said, the harsh tone gone from his voice. "I made you some soup. It'll help you relax."

"I ate already," she protested.

"What? A plastic sandwich and mud coffee?" He took her robe—a deep blue velour that matched her eyes, not the yellow bear—and nightgown from the closet, pressing them into her arms. "Change your clothes while I warm up the soup." He started toward the door, then turned to frown at her unmoving figure. "Five minutes, then I come and help you change." His grin seemed to linger behind him.

Dusty sighed and began to unbutton her blouse. She could fight his physical attractiveness or his sheltering ways. She just couldn't fight them both.

"You said you wanted to start an exercise program," Pat pointed out Saturday afternoon.

"I thought we'd be doing it outside." She'd been pedaling the exercise bike for what seemed like hours, days, weeks even, and had decided she wasn't attracted to him anymore. She hated him. He was a slave driver, a demon, a tyrant. She lifted her head enough to glare at him, but her glance caught on the firm legs, his flat stomach, those wide shoulders. Maybe hate wasn't quite accurate.

"It's raining outside." His head was bent, his eyes focused on the stopwatch in his hand.

"It'll stop someday."

He looked up, his dancing blue eyes meeting hers and sending currents of warmth through her body. "You've already missed too much with all your late hours this week. You can't afford to let the weekend go by too."

Dusty only groaned and let her gaze fall. She had decided against spending another week avoiding Pat, choosing instead to try to get him out of her system. She would spend as much time with him as possible, even resorting to the masochism of exercise. But would she survive these extra hours with him?

"Okay," Pat called out. "You've ridden from here to Dublin and back. You can stop."

"What? So soon?" She sounded more breathless than sarcastic as she got off the bike. Her legs were too wobbly to bring her close enough to Pat to take revenge. She'd rest while considering how best to pay him back. She staggered over to a chair and sank into it.

"No, no," Pat cried, coming around to pull her back up to her feet. "That's not good. You have to cool down your muscles slowly."

"I'm almost dead now," Dusty protested. "You can't be much closer to cool than that."

Pat picked up a large bath towel and wrapped it around her shoulders. "Come on, walk about a bit and then stretch."

"Pat," she pleaded. "My legs are all shaky."

"Walking will help them, and then you have to stretch."

"Swell," she grumbled. "All those years of hard work to make it in commercial real estate, and I grow up to be a rubber band."

His arm was firmly around her waist, holding her up as they walked around the room. His body was comfortable to lean against, though her legs seemed unwilling to regain their strength. What would be the point if the result was losing his support?

They padded quietly around the room, both bare-footed and in shorts and sweatshirts. His outfit was utilitarian gray, but Dusty had bought hers that week at Lord and Taylor. It consisted of robin's-egg-blue shorts, a pink short-sleeved sweatshirt, and a white headband. She had thought she looked cute in it when she started; she doubted that she did anymore. She also doubted that it mattered. That gleam probably had been surgically implanted in Pat's eye and would stay there, regardless of what she did or didn't do.

"After a hard session of cycling," Pat said, "you should always walk around a bit to cool down. That way your legs won't cramp up."

She grunted noncommittally as her left arm wrapped itself around Pat's waist. It was like grasping a tree trunk. No, a tree wouldn't be breathing. What would it be like to feel that hard strength up against her, not just pressed against her side? Her eyes drifted from reality into scenes her mind was painting. Pat slipping both his arms around her, pulling her close to his chest. Her own hands wandering over his back, feeling the rock-hard muscles, then drifting lower.

"Okay." His abruptness jarred her. "Stretch a bit and then we'll do some exercises."

Dusty was comfortable as she was. She tightened her hold a little more firmly around Pat's waist. "You do the exercises. I'll watch."

"Stretch," he ordered, removing her arm from his waist.

"I heard that you can seriously injure yourself if you do the routines improperly."

Pat put a stern mask on his face. "Miss Ross, you gave me full responsibility, in writing, for your exercise program. It was also stated, in writing, that I was not to be swayed by any pleading or crying."

"Don't worry about it," Dusty said. "I'll take full responsibility."

The stern mask didn't soften. "That's not the way I'm made, Miss Ross. I accepted the resonsibility. I'll fulfill it."

Reluctantly she stretched, then went on to his exercises and other routines using two-and-a-half-pound dumbbells he'd gotten specially for her.

Dumbbell, that was her all right. She stared up at the blue weights as she lay on her back, lifting her arms from the floor to over her head. Why had she let herself fall for a guy who would never return her interest?

Dumbbells up. "How come you never married, Pat?" Dumbbells down.

"On a butler's salary?"

Dumbbells up. "You haven't always been a butler. Surely you made more playing soccer." Dumbbells down.

"And never really had a home either. Not a settled one for a family."

Up. "Oh, come on. That can't have bothered others. There must be plenty of married soccer players." Down.

"I'm not other men," he pointed out. "I'm not going to marry until I earn enough to support a wife."

Up. "Maybe she could support you." Down.

"No. A man takes care of his own." He reached down and took the dumbbells from her hands. "Enough of those. Pushups now."

She turned over. Maybe it was Pat's old-fashioned approach that made him so endearing: his gentle courtesies, his air of protection, his pampering ways. That thought almost made her laugh aloud. This exercise session was not what she would have thought of as pampering, yet she had to admit that the workout was making her feel great. She was tingling, alive and full of energy.

Pat's hand came down on her back. "No, you've got to keep straighter here. Make your arms and shoulders do the work."

The spot he touched seemed to burn even long after his hand was gone. Maybe it wasn't the exercises but the coach that was affecting her. She did her situps, then lay back, eyes closed, arms and legs outstretched. How did she go about attracting his attention?

"Good job, Miss Ross," Pat said. "Why don't you take a shower? I'll be starting dinner soon."

Dusty didn't even blink. A good coach would make sure she took a proper shower. And offer to wash her back if she were too tired.

"Miss Ross?"

She didn't smile, though the worried tone in his

voice almost broke her resolve. Her big, tough drill sergeant was worried. Satisfaction spread a comforting balm over her tired limbs. Some other sensation was also creeping in.

"Camilla?"

His voice was suddenly closer, and she slid one eyelid open to find him kneeling next to her, his worried face close to hers. The giggle she had imprisoned broke its bonds and escaped her lips.

"That wasn't nice," he scolded. "You had me worried."

"Good," she said. "You worked me close to death." This time several giggles spilled forth in laughter.

The boyish frown on his brow awoke within her a devilish need to tease along with a burning hunger for closeness. He was on his knees, leaning over her, arms on either side of her body. Her fingers moved up to dance across his ribs and the words "Are you ticklish?" tumbled from her mouth.

Her touch caused him to crumple and collapse, his chest across hers, his weight heavy but wonderful. His hands reached out to imprison hers.

"You're being very naughty," he said.

"Oh?" Her fingers tried to squirm away from him. They liked the feel of his body and were ready to do more exploring but his hold on her was tight.

His eyes were just inches away, the laughing gleam gone, replaced by a deeper, darker flame. Slowly his head came down and their lips met in a gentle embrace. A fleeting brush, the wind gently caressing the flowers, the moon silvering the night.

The answering flame within her was neither gentle nor mild. It consumed her with the suddenness of sunshine, the wonder of spring. She searched his eyes for some hint, some sign that he had felt that hunger too. For a moment she thought his eyes had darkened with the power of a summer storm, but then he turned away.

Pat pushed himself up abruptly, his eyes staring off, away from her. "I'd better get dinner started." He helped her up. His touch was brief, but enough. She could feel his needs, his wants, and his confusion.

"You're sweated up. You'd better shower quickly before you get chilled." He turned and was gone.

Chilled? Not likely. The fires raging in her were too strong for that.

"You are one super-daft bastard," Pat growled through clenched teeth at the broad Irish face staring back at him. He emphasized each word with a vigorous brush stroke to the unruly thatch of hair on his head.

He threw the brush down on the sink ledge. That was the best he could do. His hair was growing too long. He fixed the errant strands with a fierce glower. Monday they'd be cut back to size.

It wasn't just his hair that needed cutting back to size, and he knew it. What in heaven's name had ever possessed him? She was his employer and here he was coveting her like a shy lad sneaking a kiss before church. Fool!

The open-necked shirt and the short sleeves straining to circle his biceps caught his eye. What the hell was he doing now? He looked like he was dressed for darts and a pint or two with the lads. He tore the shirt off and went into his bedroom. He was a butler and a butler always dressed properly.

He put on a long-sleeved shirt and a black bow tie. This job was nothing but an invitation to trouble. A pretty young woman with twinkling eyes and himself without any health problems. At times his ankles were a bit tender, but that didn't seem to affect his glands. Trouble, hell. It was an invitation to disaster.

The long-sleeved shirt looked better, but for good measure he covered it with a short-waisted white jacket. He replaced his loafers with black shiny wing tips.

Turning before the mirror, Pat examined his formality. "That should throw a little water on the flames," he said.

His image did not comment, but displeasure still ruled his facial muscles. Changing his style of dress was a start, but only that. The real problem lay in his head—and other parts of his body. Camilla was his employer, not just a pretty lass with lips that needed kissing. He had to stop seeing her smile in his dreams. He had to stop trying to slay the dragons that threatened her and keep his mind on his work. To convince himself of his determination to do just that and only that, he marched into the kitchen to get started on dinner.

"Damn," he muttered under his breath when he saw the clock. All that fooling around with his uniform had made him late. He quickly got the chicken into the oven to bake and pulled the salad greens from the refrigerator.

The light humming floating down from Camilla's room tensed his shoulders, but he made himself relax. She could hum all she liked. It didn't bother him. He hardly noticed it.

He took out the dishes and set a place at the kitchen table. No, that wasn't how it should be either. He took the dishes and carried them into the dining room. Camilla should not be eating in the same place that he was working. She deserved her privacy. It was only proper.

He checked the chicken, started some wild rice cooking, and then put lettuce, tomatoes, a celery stalk, and a cucumber on the butcher-block counter-top. The lettuce was torn and he had just picked up the slicing knife when Camilla's presence invaded the kitchen. He did not turn. He was a butler, not some lovestruck lad. The sudden warmth of his brow was due to standing near the oven.

"Wow, fancy," she purred. "Do I have guests that I don't know about?"

"I'm sure you don't, madam." The tomato was cut into precise slices.

He heard the light shuffling of skin on tile. Camilla hadn't bothered to put her shoes on. Not that it mattered. He'd seen bare feet and more, both as a butler and as a man. Pat clenched his teeth, and the grinding echoed in his empty head. All he had to concentrate on now was his butler half. Butlers saw a lot of things, but never got involved. They were tough that way. He was tough that way. He pitched the tomatoes to their doom in the salad.

He reached for the cucumber and caught a glimpse of Camilla standing near him. She was wearing a pair of deep blue lounging pajamas that set off the sapphire glow of her eyes and the reddish highlights in her hair. The soft material clung to her form gently, like snow clings to a branch, like raindrops cling to a petal. Like a wise butler clings to his principles. He concentrated on the cucumber.

"Are you going out tonight?" someone else asked using his voice.

"No." She reached over to sneak a cucumber slice

and popped it into her mouth. "I'm free as a bird. No hot, passionate dates on the horizon."

"I'm sorry to hear that, ma'am." That was a damn lie. The only thing he was sorry about was the terms of their relationship. If they had met in normal circumstances, she wouldn't be a free little bird at all. She'd be his. Imprisoned in the cage of his passion.

"Do you want me to set the table?" she asked.

"No," he mumbled, shaking his head. "I've already set your place in the dining room."

"That's dumb," she said. "Why should I eat alone?"

She left the room and he pitched the cucumber slices down among the carnage of the tomatoes. Then he clenched his fists and took a deep breath. Easy, lad.

Camilla returned with the place setting and put it on the kitchen table. "Want me to set a place for you?"

"No, thank you, madam." Pat slowly exhaled. He was in control now.

She sat down but she was still too near. He pulled at his collar slightly. He'd be glad when he could turn that damn oven off."

"Sure I can't help?" she asked.

"Quite sure." He put her salad into a small glass bowl and placed it in front of her. "What would madam like on her salad?"

"I don't know." She went to the refrigerator and opened the door, peering inside. "I'll find something."

Her lip was stuck out in a little-girl pout, and he found himself staring at her and the clinging pajamas. Damn shame to let some silk rags do all the clutching and clinging. He could do a better job with one hand tied behind his back.

Double, triple, and quadruple damn. She didn't

know the first thing about having a butler. She was too young to have one. The oven buzzer sounded and Pat irritably went to take the chicken out before she decided to do that too. He placed the pan on the counter to cool.

"I'll have creamy Italian."

"Very good, madam." He tried to take the bottle from her, but she slid away from him with a laugh.

"No, let me do it. Let's see if that weight training is doing any good." She opened the bottle and raised her arms in triumph. "Success," she exclaimed. "How's that for macho?"

Pat spooned a bed of rice onto the plate and then placed a breast of chicken on it. She wasn't macho at all. She was a fragile little wisp of a girl, ready to take on the world. She was a tiny kitten thinking its claws were protection. He puttered about uneasily, waiting for her to finish her salad.

"When do you eat?" she asked.

He found a speck of dirt on the counter and carefully annihilated it. "After you finish," he said once he was through.

"You'd waste less time if you ate with me."

"I'm not comfortable eating while I work."

"Suit yourself."

He put the chicken down in front of her, the plate slipping and hitting the table with a slight thud. Lord, he couldn't do that. Suiting himself would mean taking her into his arms and crushing her to him until she groaned in ecstasy. If he did that, he'd either be in jail or have his job classification changed to gigolo. Neither would do. No woman ever put a Mahoney in jail or on a leash.

*   *   *

Camilla jabbed at the television button, wiping the picture of the laughing faces from the screen. She could hear Pat cleaning up the kitchen and frowned. After that brief glimpse of heaven this afternoon, she'd hoped they'd be soaring past the clouds by this time. But Pat was not cooperating.

She picked up a book she'd bought earlier in the week, but only got as far as the first searing kiss the Irish warrior hero bestowed upon the heroine's trembling lips before she tossed the book aside in disgust. She thought she heard footsteps approaching and grabbed up a copy of *Business Week*.

"Do you have any preferences for breakfast or dinner tomorrow, Miss Ross?"

Dusty put her magazine down and looked up over the tops of her reading glasses at the gorgeous man in front of her. The Irish warrior for whom her lips were trembling. He did not seem to be trembling for her with quite the same eagerness though. What would he say if she chose him for breakfast?"

"No, I don't really care."

"How about flounder for dinner and eggs Benedict for breakfast?"

"Sounds fine."

"Very good, madam." He turned to leave without subduing any of the desires warring within her.

"Pat, are you angry with me?"

He stopped, his shoulders rigid, his body tense as his eyes stared down at the floor. "No, madam. I'm not." His face came up again, hardened as if bitter winds whipped around him. Or in him. "I'm angry with myself. I'm sorry if that spilled over on to you."

His hair fell over his forehead. Her hands longed to brush it back and ruffle it some more.

"I enjoyed my exercise session today," she said.

"I apologize for my indiscretion, madam." The words were rushed, a bitter job best done quickly.

"There's nothing to apologize for. It was something we both wanted."

"Perhaps it would be better if I—"

A panic froze her heart, and she got her words out ahead of whatever drastic offers he was about to make. "Look, it happened and it's over. We're adults, let's act like grownups."

His eyes did not seem able or willing to meet hers. Just as well, for she was reflecting on the various ways adults could act.

"As you wish, ma'am."

As she wished? No, not quite, but it was what she'd have to settle for at the moment until she could think of some way to melt through his reserve again.

"Is there anything else, madam?"

"No, good night, Pat."

"Good night, madam." His eyes remained distant and he left the room.

Dusty stared at the space where he had stood and watched thin air take the form of her wild Irish warrior.

"Oh, my," she muttered as she stood up and reached for her book. Maybe it was time to see what came after the earth-shattering kiss. It would be nice to be prepared, just in case.

Six

"Hi, Dad. Got any use for three tickets to an indoor soccer game tonight?" Dusty asked, absently building a paper-clip chain while she spoke into the phone. "Somebody got them for a client but then couldn't use them after all."

"Friday's a good night to go out. We can make an evening of it."

"We? I thought you'd want to take some friends."

"Aren't you my friend?"

"Dad," Dusty protested.

"Which is it, Camilla? You got a date or you don't want to go out with your old man?"

"There are three tickets, Dad. Who else are you going to invite?"

"Bring your butler. He's a big soccer nut, played indoor and outdoor himself. For San Diego or someplace like that."

That was no guarantee Pat would want to spend an

evening with her. It had been thirteen days since he'd kissed her and she still hadn't found a chink in his armor, a crack in his wall, a weak link in his chain. She frowned and threw down her paper clips. "I'm not sure he'd want to come."

"I didn't say to ask him. Hell. Doesn't he work for you? Give him an order. Tell him he's got to come along to carry your coat and open the door or something like that."

She seemed incapable of doing anything but rleasing a sigh. They'd kept on with her exercise program, but she might have been wearing an overcoat instead of new leotards or new shorts for all Pat noticed. He'd become a frozen statue and barely even met her eyes, let alone noticed the hunger in them. Damn. She was living with the greatest guy she'd ever met. But was ordering him to attend a soccer game with her a move in the right direction?

"I'll drive," her father went on. "A buddy of mine told me about a new Polish place over on Central Avenue. Super food, cheap prices. See you guys at five."

Dusty found herself with a dead line and an open mouth. She rectified both situations and picked up the phone to call Pat.

"Don't crowd the driver, Camilla," her father said.

"I'll put my arm up here," Pat offered, and placed his arm on the back of the seat. He turned his bulk slightly sideways, leaning against the door. "That'll make more room."

"Sorry," Camilla murmured. She wasn't sorry at having to move closer to Pat, but because her nearness seemed so abhorrent to him.

She stared straight ahead at the dull cityscape.

Even spring didn't bring color to the tired buildings lining the broken and beaten streets slowly shuffling by them. But then, spring couldn't work miracles. It certainly wasn't working any on Pat's mood. When he had first come to work for her he was lighthearted, cheerful. Now he had all the joy of a snowstorm in April. Tonight he was overcast, with a strong probability of freezing rain.

Dinner had been awful. Her stuffed beef roll was delicious, but she couldn't eat much. Pat's appetite didn't seem affected, but his manner was stiff and formal. Her father not only had to carry the conversation, he had to resuscitate it every few minutes. She shouldn't have made Pat come.

"Wish you two would quiet down," her father grumbled, slashing at the silence. "It's hard enough driving in this traffic without you yakking nonstop."

Dusty felt her cheeks warm. Her father sounded just as he had when he'd driven her and little Jimmy Shea, from across the alley, to band practice. Except then they had had the luxury of having the whole backseat to themselves, Jimmy by one window and she across the car by the other. Tonight her father's backseat was piled up with boxes. Some odds and ends he said he kept forgetting to drop off at the Salvation Army store.

Pat cleared his throat. "Should be a good game."

"Yeah," her father agreed.

"The two teams are tied for first place." Dusty had done her homework and read the newspaper.

After a long moment Pat cleared his throat again. "We always hated playing the Sting at home."

"I imagine," her father said, turning to look across her at Pat. "They don't lose too many at the old stadium."

"They can be completely exhausted," Pat said. "Then comes the fourth quarter and ten or fifteen thousand people start screaming and they come on like a fresh team."

"Does a crowd really make that much difference for professional players?" Dusty asked.

"Oh, sure," Pat said. "Every professional entertainer works better with a loving audience. You can feel the emotion reaching out to you."

Couldn't he feel her emotions reaching out to him? She stared straight ahead, willing to be his loving audience if he'd let her.

They parked in a cinder lot and walked the block to the stadium door. Around them were young couples on dates, parents with their kids, and various assorted fans, all looking happy and excited. Even Pat's face was alight and his voice animated as he and her father discussed the merits of the two teams. Was she the only one who didn't care who won the game? How could she even concentrate on it when Pat seemed blind to the fact that she was a woman?

Their seats were great, down close to the field, but high enough to see the action. They settled in to watch a pregame match between two high school girls teams. Pat's arm brushed against hers, but her eyes remained glued to the field. She knew little about soccer and nothing about how it was played indoors, but it didn't matter. Her eyes were seeing the play down on the field, but her body knew only that Pat was close. That his arm was touching hers, that his voice was washing over her as he spoke to her father, that she wanted to move her hand slightly to touch his.

"Ever see an indoor game before?"

She almost jumped, so startled was she to feel his

gentle breath against her ear. Of course, the stadium was noisy. He'd have to lean close to be heard. She turned to face him. His eyes were deep and immediate, a fire burning in them that his voice didn't reveal. Confusion spilled over her, and she chose just to answer his question.

"I've never even seen an outdoor game."

His smile sent sparks through the air that fell onto her cheeks and ignited them. "You've got a real treat ahead of you, then."

He turned to face the rink, still leaning close, and pointed out different parts of the playing field. She knew his enthusiasm was for the game he loved, not because she was with him, but it was hard—no impossible—not to catch some of his fever.

He took her hand in his, though she doubted he was even aware of it. She tried not to clutch at him and hoped that her answers were intelligible. They weren't to her, but he kept on talking, so she must have made some sense.

The girls' game finished, the lights went off except for a spotlight that caught a huge bumblebee prancing around the field. Pat dropped her hand to applaude, and she joined him and the thousands of other fans.

"See, aren't you glad you decided to come?" her father asked, leaning close to her.

"Yeah, Dad. It's great." At least for the next few hours Pat would be next to her. No running away, no hiding behind a cold wooden exterior. She'd share his enthusiasm for the game and his elbow space. Maybe the fire raging through her would spread.

"Oh, that feels wonderful," Dusty exclaimed after

she had downed half a stein of beer. The cool liquid was soothing to her ravaged vocal cords. "The least I'll be tomorrow is hoarse, I'll be lucky if I have any voice."

"Send a prayer heavenward, Pat," her father said out of the side of his mouth. "Maybe you'll get lucky and she won't."

"Don't be a smart aleck," she snapped. She tried to punch her father's shoulder, but she was squeezed between the two men in the tavern booth and it was hard to put any power behind the motion.

"And I don't want even a smile out of you," she said, turning on Pat.

"I'm solemn as a bishop, madam."

She smiled at him, glad that their gentle teasing was back to what it had been in the beginning. She took another long drink of her beer and leaned back against the hard wooden bench, relaxed between the two muscular men. She felt cozy and protected and happy. "I still can't believe how much I yelled."

"Ask my right ear," Pat said.

"They needed me," she said. "You said yourself that the fans are very important."

"Can't argue with you there," Pat agreed. "They did win."

"They smashed the other team," she corrected him. "They obliterated them. Ten to four is more than just winning."

Pat turned and called across her. "Has she always been this bloodthirsty?"

"Always," her father answered.

"I resent that," Dusty scolded. "I am and have always been a gentle lady."

"That's why I don't take her places anymore," her father put in. "It was okay when I was young. I was always a little too heavy to run fast, but I could handle the trouble that she and her mother brought on us."

"We were always ladies." Dusty sniffed.

"But now," he continued, "on top of being too fat to run, I'm too old to fight." He took a healthy swig of his beer. "All I got left is being nice, and my heart's too weak to take that kind of radical change."

"You were rowdy because you wanted to be," Dusty grumbled. "Don't blame me."

She drained her glass of beer and sat relaxed in the cocoon that the two bulky men on either side of her provided. The noise was loud, but not intrusive. She gazed idly at her empty glass. Should she call the waitress? Pat's glass was low too. Maybe he'd want another himself and could get her a refill while getting one of his own.

"Hey, Pat," her father called. "Do me a favor?"

"Sure."

"Take Camilla out on the dance floor. That blond in the green blouse over on the near side of the bar has been giving me the eye for the past ten minutes. I've got the available sign out, but Camilla here is confusing her."

"What?" Dusty exclaimed, and peered through the dimly lit room toward the bar. She could barely see the bar, let alone a woman in a green blouse.

"Let's dance, Camilla," Pat said even as he pulled her to her feet.

"Pat!" But it was only a token protest and she let him draw her close once they reached the even darker dance floor.

The juke box was wailing out slow, sensuous music that urged her nearer to him. She had no will but to relax against him.

His body was strong and powerful, his arms

placing her in a captivity she willingly submitted to. She laid her head against his chest, feeling and hearing the pounding of his heart.

She took a deep breath, almost shuddering from the pure pleasure of being so close to him. His arms brought a wonderful sense of peace and safety to her, a closeness that they shared, just the two of them, a haven away from the rest of the world.

True, she had sat next to him in the car and at the stadium, but this was so wonderfully different. Here, his arms were holding her by choice. It didn't matter that it was her father's suggestion. Her father hadn't dictated the degree of closeness, he hadn't decreed that their hearts beat in unison.

Pat's hands spread over her back, pulling her nearer to him with possessive certainty, though their bodies seemed already melted together. Her eyes were shut, but her senses were filled with him. The smell of his soap embraced her, the rough hair of his chest tickled her cheek right through his shirt, and the sound of his unsteady breathing mingled with their heartbeats. Her mind held confused images of time and place, but none of that mattered as long as their arms refused to release each other. Their bodies moved as one, as if they'd danced forever together, and maybe they had. In spirit, if not in body.

All too soon their communion ended. Dusty felt confused and alone as Pat's arms slowly dropped from her and the dance floor returned. It took her a moment to realize the music had stopped. Was it only that? Had she only imagined the soulful melodies humming between them?

The music started up again. "Now that we have the kinks worked out, we might as well enjoy it," Pat whispered to her.

"We might as well," Dusty agreed, and melted into his embrace again.

She lost count of the songs, only knowing that she and Pat were close, moving with sensuous rhythm to the hungers of their souls which coincidentally matched the outside rhythms of the music. Pat's breath was soft and warm on her hair, and from time to time his lips seemed to brush the top of her head. Was she imagining it? Was it part of her dreams? Had wanting him so brought delusions of happiness?

She no longer cared whether it was reality or not. All she wanted was for the dancing and pausing to go on. Dance and pause. Dance and pause. It was heaven to be held in those arms and then stare up into those eyes, their fires glowing even in the darkness. She was about to give the rest of her life to the rhythm when she was jarred by a bump. Dusty looked up and frowned into the smiling eyes of her father. Before she could say anything he floated away.

"Care for a refill on that beer?" Pat asked.

"Sure." She felt cold without his arms around her and foolish for having woven a spell that had enchanted only her. "I guess you occupied me well enough to give Dad his chance with the blonde."

"Oh, that's me all right," he said with a laugh, and led her through the crowd. "Willing to sacrifice and hold a beautiful lady in my arms just to give a friend a chance."

Some of the worry and bitterness fled with her laughter. They stopped at the bar and got two more beers, then Pat carried them back to the booth.

"I could have carried mine," she said, sinking into the shadowy privacy of their booth. He put her mug in front of her and sat down around the corner of the table from her.

"Why? I am your butler."

She'd chosen to ignore that fact all evening. Why couldn't he? "Can't we pretend you aren't? How about if I give you the evening off?"

He shook his head slowly, but it wasn't in answer to her question. "I'm still your butler, even on my evenings off."

She looked at him, her gaze touching his lips, the firmness of his cheek, and lingering on the sadness in his eyes. He looked back for a long moment, then stared into his mug.

"Does it have to matter?" she asked. His hand was so close, her fingers strayed to lightly touch the dark hairs on its back.

He withstood her gentle tickling for only an instant, then covered her hand with his. The pressure was hard, and warm, and sad, clinging because it was impossible not to. But it was also impossible to continue. "How can it not matter?" he asked.

She started to protest and he covered her lips with his finger. Emboldened by hungers too strong to ignore and fearful of his protests, she kissed it and smiled. He smiled back.

"You're a fine lady," he told her. "And I respect you as well as like you. It's just not wise to let things grow between us."

"Maybe it's too late to stop it."

His smile almost reached his eyes. "I can see why you're so good at your job. You never give up, do you?"

"No." With her free hand she played with her beer, turning the mug slightly, watching the amber liquid slosh about. She looked up suddenly and caught his hungry gaze on her. "What's so terrible about enjoying each other's company? Can't we still laugh together if you're my butler?"

"I've been dreaming of a bit more than laughing with you," he admitted.

Her sense of power grew. She leaned closer to him, her free hand encircling his. "So have I."

His hands fled to grasp his mug of beer. "You're missing the purpose of the game and just thinking of scoring goals."

He didn't look up and missed her grin.

"I'm a butler and you, better than anybody, know just how much money I make. Not enough for a future. Not enough for more than a few casual dates." His glower was fierce and wild. "And don't suggest a raise."

The problems she hadn't seen were now perfectly evident. "Pat, I like you. I enjoy your company. Can't we just relax and let the future take care of itself?"

His frown seemed chiseled in stone. "I'm thinking that maybe I should quit."

"No!"

"I may be a butler, but I'm also a man," he went on. His voice was a harsh whisper. "Back in Europe all my employers were older women. Nice women with families. Not the object of my dreams like you've become. I'm thinking, for your sake it'd be best if I quit."

"For my sake?" This was worse than she'd expected.

"It was too nice out there on the dance floor with you in my arms. What if I should slip someday, being there alone with you all the time?"

She couldn't believe that he was saying. "Pat, you can't quit. I won't let you."

Before he could answer, her father returned to the

table. Dusty was half-glad and half-mad at the interruption. Maybe it was for the best. It gave her a reprieve and time to think of a way to get through to Pat. He was attracted to her; that much she knew now. It shouldn't be too hard to get him to act on that attraction.

"You're sure you don't mind my bunking here for the night?"

"Of course not, Dad. It's too long a drive home for you this late at night." She put the pile of sheets and blankets on the sofa. "Got everything you need?"

"Looks like it." He tossed a few of the decorative pillows over onto a chair. "I wouldn't want to put a crimp in your plans, you know."

Laughter erupted easily, bubbling over the surface to bring a smile to her father's eyes. "No, Dad, you're not." How could he even ask that after the stiff, silent ride home?

"You can tell me to go. I'll understand."

She hugged him. "In spite of all your matchmaking this evening, Pat is still just my butler."

A wave of red washed over his cheeks. "I was just trying to help. He's a nice guy and it's time you settled down with somebody."

"Yes, sir. I'll go tell him that." She kissed his cheek. "Sleep well."

"G'night, Camilla."

She hadn't lied. She was glad her father was here tonight. Pat would figure her virtue was safe while her father was in the apartment, and by the time Dad left tomorrow, she hoped Pat would have forgotten all that nonsense about quitting.

Pat appeared at the other end of the hall. "Uh, good

night, Miss Ross. Does your father have everything he needs?"

"Yes, thank you. I think he's settling in for the night."

"And yourself, ma'am? Is there anything else I can do for you?"

She behaved and shoved all the wonderful ideas that invaded her mind back into oblivion. "No, thank you, Pat. See you tomorrow."

"Good night, ma'am."

Seven

"It's a great old building," Mr. Ross told Pat over coffee the next morning. "And in a terrific location. I think it'd be perfect for what you want."

"Sounds almost too good to be true." Pat stared down into his coffee cup, his mind alive with the possibilities. If he could find the right location, if he could actually get his dream off the ground, he could start living like a real person instead of putting up with this straitjacket existence he had now. Look, but don't see. See, but don't touch. Living with Camilla was driving him up the wall.

"What do you say we take a look at it early next week?" Mr. Ross suggested.

"The sooner the better."

"Morning, all." Dusty came into the room looking fresh and clean as a field of daisies. She was wearing a pale yellow short-sleeve blouse and jeans that demolished the little resolve Pat had left where she was concerned. He got to his feet and cleared the breakfast dishes off the table, not allowing his eyes to stray past the bare feet peeking out below her jeans.

"Good morning, Miss Ross. How would an omelette suit you this morning?"

"What's this 'Miss Ross' business?" her father asked. "After all the cuddling you two were doing on that dance floor last night, you ought to have gotten beyond that."

"Good morning to you too, Daddy." She kissed his cheek and sat down in the chair next to him. "An omelette will be fine, Pat."

Her voice was light and lilting, a teasing song that called out to him like the strains of the ancient Greek sirens. Pat set the frying pan roughly on the burner. He wasn't one of Ulysses's sailors. He got out the eggs and carefully kept his back to Camilla.

"Nice of you to get up finally," her father grumbled. "It's almost lunchtime, and we ate hours ago."

"What's wrong with sleeping late on Saturday? We were out past midnight and I was tired. Besides"— her eyes seized Pat's as he brought her orange juice over—"I was having such wonderful dreams, I didn't want to wake up."

Pat retreated to the counter and beat the eggs until the fever in his blood eased. When his business venture started moving he'd quit this job and come back to accept the challenge that spilled from Camilla's eyes. He'd fuel that teasing until it turned into a flame of desire.

"Coffee, Miss Ross?"

"Hey, she spends enough time on her high horse already," her father snorted. "Her name's Camilla. Try it. Ca-mil-la."

Her blue eyes dared him, sparkling like cool mountain lakes. She was playing a game that he could play just as well.

"Coffee, Camilla?" The name rolled off his tongue sweet as honey.

"Yes, thank you." The mountain lakes warmed.

While Camilla and her father chatted, Pat made her omelette. Camilla, Camilla, Camilla. He liked the way her name sounded when he said it out loud. He liked the warmth that filled her eyes. He slid the omelette onto a plate and served it, then refilled his and Mr. Ross's cups before he sat back down.

"Do you have enough room there?" Mr. Ross asked Pat. "Why don't we squeeze closer to Camilla? A little thing like her doesn't need much room."

"Maybe you two would like me to sit out on the front steps?"

"No, ma'am." Pat smiled at her and then corrected himself. "No, Camilla." He lingered long enough on her name to bring dusky streaks into her cheeks and then smiled into his coffee. A little of her own mischief back and she'd be a bit more respectful.

"We like having a little sweetheart like you around," her father assured her. "Ain't that right, Pat?"

He made his smile as smooth and rich as cream. "We most certainly do."

"I appreciate your enthusiasm."

"Now, Camilla," her father said, patting her on the leg. "Be nice."

She gave her father an irritated look, but he returned a surprised one. "Boy," he said. "You're really firming up." His eyes moved up to her shoulders. "You have a squarer set to your shoulders too. What have you been doing, exercising for a change?"

"Pat's developed an exercise program for me," she said.

"That's a good idea," her father told Pat. "She was getting kind of flabby, wasn't she?"

Pat sipped at his coffee. "More on the thin side actually."

"Yeah, in her upper body," Dusty Senior agreed. "But down around the middle, flab city, as my nephew's young son would say."

This time Pat took a healthy swallow of coffee. "It was a bit on the soft side," he said. "But not unpleasantly so."

Two pairs of blue eyes stared at him, one pair mocking, the other overcast and stormy. Lesser men might consider striking sails and sitting out the storm in some safe harbor, but Mahoneys were made of stern stuff.

"It's a little early to see the improvement," Mr. Ross said, his hand on Camilla's shoulder. "But you really can feel it."

Pat took another sip of coffee and emptied the cup. Unfortunately getting up now to refill it would seem like retreat, like cowardice. He ignored the danger rumbling in the distance.

"Well, can you?" Camilla asked. Her voice had a peculiar echoing quality that he hadn't noticed before, and her eyes were filled with little glittering specks. A quick glance confirmed his suspicions. The glittering specks were sparks, sparks from a raging forest fire.

He cleared his throat and tried to douse the flames with a cool professionalism. "I beg your pardon, madam?"

Her lips curved into smile. "I asked if *you* can feel the improvement?"

There was no mistaking the challenge in her voice or the screams of his Irish ancestors demanding that he pick up her gauntlet. For the Mahoney honor, for the pride of family, for the sake of the generations yet unborn that would have to carry the burden of shame if he proved cowardly, he took a deep breath and reached over to feel her shoulder. "Yes," he agreed. "It's coming along quite well. Indeed it is."

Embers glowed in Camilla's eyes and Pat pushed back his chair slightly. There was a difference between cowardice and good sense. He'd get his coffee now before an answering fire raged inside him.

"Is there anything else you'd like him to check out, Dad?" The question was directed at her father, but Camilla's eyes were still on Pat.

"You're pectorals look better too," Mr. Ross said. "What do you think, Pat?"

The hell with good sense. "I think I'll pass on that." Pat retreated to the stove.

"Chicken."

Those ancestral ghosts rose up again in horror. Chicken? Had she really called a Mahoney chicken? The idea was so preposterous that he pushed the screaming spirits back. They must have misunderstood.

"Your waist is nice," her father continued. "But I was attached to those little love handles you had."

Pat came slowly back to the table and refilled everyone's cup as Camilla ate the last of her omelette.

"That was delicious, Pat." Her voice was almost normal. "You sure have a way with eggs."

A gloating smile was in her eyes as well as on her lips, and his ancestors shrieked for vengeance. They allowed him to put the coffeepot back on the stove, then armed him for battle. A pure Irish smile of innocence was put on his lips, the wit of the Mahoneys was on his tongue, and the charm of generations danced in his eyes.

He moved his chair around the corner of the table and slid into it. Camilla's eyes narrowed with suspicion as he slipped his arm around her waist. "Fits real good," he said with a hearty laugh, and pulled his arm a little tighter. She settled against him snugly, her soft fragrance filling the air. "Fits perfectly, in fact."

"I'm so glad," she murmured, and tried to ease away from him.

He smiled and refused to budge as his other hand slid over her thigh, checking it out through the snug-fitting denim. "Thigh feels top-notch too," Pat assured her, and then moved his hand down her leg slowly. Down the thigh, over the knee, and around to the calf. Her eyes darkened. "And those calf muscles." He shook his head sadly. "They'd tempt St. Patrick himself into sin."

Her father was trying hard not to laugh. "You're doing one helluva job here, Pat."

"Thank you, sir. I certainly try to do my best. My dear departed mother, may God bless her soul, instilled a sense of duty and discipline into all her boys."

He sat up and reluctantly let go of Camilla's waist. After moving his chair back, he sipped at his coffee. His ancestors receded. The silence that followed seemed heavy and explosive in spite of Dusty Senior's chuckling. Pat could still feel Camilla's leg beneath his hand. He wanted to try it all again, but this time without the denim barrier. He took another sip of coffee, but even the hot, bitter taste wasn't distracting.

"More coffee, Dad?" Her voice was almost normal. Pat forced himself to look into her eyes and found them dark and smoldering, like a fire built with green wood, but she didn't seem exactly angry.

Her father got to his feet and leaned over to kiss her cheek. "Two cups is my limit, honey. I have a lot of chores, so I'd better run. Thanks for everything." She got to her feet, too, and he put an affectionate arm around her. "You know what's so great about this little girl?" he asked Pat. "You can always kid around with her."

Pat allowed himself only a quick glance at Camilla. That strange look was still in her eyes. He searched about for support, only to find that his ancestors had left. Every one of them had scurried away, taking that famous Mahoney charm with them and leaving only the fire that had produced all the subsequent generations. It was time for a cold shower or some heavy weight training.

He and Camilla escorted Mr. Ross to the door. "Don't do all the cleaning up yourself," he told Pat. "You might as well get some use out of her muscles."

Camilla laughed, a full, hearty laugh that sent cold shivers up his spine. He wasn't against a good laugh now and then himself, but Pat didn't think that the brightness in her eyes came from the sunshine of joy.

As the door closed after Mr. Ross, Pat's body went on the alert. The next few minutes could be a bit tricky. "I'll clean up," he said.

"How sweet."

"I want to make sure you get your money's worth."

"I intend to."

Her dangerous smile reminded him of the lack of little Mahoneys to carry on the name, and his duty to rectify the situation, but his feet somehow kept him going into the kitchen. There he immersed his hands in steaming hot, soapy dishwater. The pain was severe, but it didn't drown out the nagging of his ancestors, who had suddenly reappeared.

Dusty took her time. If there was one thing she had learned in real estate, it was that timing was everything. A piece of property could be worth thousands one week and millions the next. It was all timing.

She heard Pat doing the dishes in the kitchen and started on her accounting homework. Halfway through her history assignment she heard him begin his weight training and smiled. The time was getting closer. She finished her history and paged through the novel she'd been reading. The trembling heroine had been torn from her Irish warrior's arms. He probably hadn't been exercising with her, or she would have been strong enough to do more than sob. Dusty looked up from the book. No sound was coming from Pat's rooms.

A deliciously wicked feeling came over her as she strolled down the hall. Her dad was safe from her revenge, but Pat wasn't. He didn't have any way to escape her. She was going to make him pay for his teasing and more. Today he was going to feel the same hunger that had been eating at her. She heard the sound of his shower as she sat down on the weight bench. When the water was turned off she tapped lightly at the bathroom door.

"I'd like a word with you, please," she called in to him.

His light humming stopped and a moment later, with only a towel wrapped around his middle, he came out. Confusion and consternation raced like warring demons over his face.

A feeling of pity surfaced like the first crocus of

spring, but Dusty examined it and found it wanting. She tore the piteous feeling out by the roots, throwing it aside. He deserved no mercy.

"I'll be with you in a minute, Miss Ross," he said. "Just let me get dressed and I'll come find you."

"My, aren't we polite?" A jungle cat moving in on its helpless prey, she took a step closer to him.

"I'm always polite, madam. At least, I always try to be."

"Always?" She moved even closer and circled slightly around him, enjoying his obvious attempt to keep her in view. "How would you classify that session at breakfast today? Very polite, medium polite, or slightly polite?"

A grin split Pat's face and washed away all evidence of concern. "That was just a bit of friendly humor. There was no lack of respect intended."

"Well, it wasn't very fair."

"Fair?" The intensity of his smile dimmed somewhat, but confusion, not concern, danced in his eyes. "Fathers always tease their little girls. That's how they show them that they love them."

"To the best of my knowledge, I have only one father."

Pat raked a hand through his hair; his other hand was busy holding the edges of his towel together securely. "Well, brothers tend to do the same thing."

"I don't have any brothers. In fact, I'm an only child." She was behind him now, and he was forced to keep glancing over his shoulder.

He shrugged. "The term can be used loosely. You know, it includes men who feel close to you in a brotherly sort of way."

"So if brothers can tease a sister, it ought to be fair for sisters to tease a brother, right?"

"Yes," he agreed slowly. "That's only fair."

"I'm glad you agree." She smiled and came around in front of him. "Because I'd like to perform the same test on you. I'd like to help you in the same way you helped me."

"Oh?"

She was waiting for panic to seize him, but he just blinked once and somehow turned his face to stone. His eyes were fixed on a spot somewhere beyond her. She didn't let disappointment undercut her determination.

"I mean, you may be exercising to no avail," she pointed out. "You really need someone to let you know how you're doing." The pounding in her eardrums was so great, she wouldn't have heard his reply had he made one, but she watched his lips. They didn't move.

She took a deep breath and willed herself to go on. She'd gotten this far; she couldn't back down. And to be honest, there was only one small voice inside her warning caution, and it was easy to ignore. She put her hands on his shoulders, squeezing them slightly. "Very firm," she assessed. "I'd say rock-hard."

Her hands slid down his arms from the shoulders, across his still-damp skin. "Biceps are beautiful." She remembered the strength of his hold last night when they'd been dancing. Those biceps were more than beautiful, they were perfect. They were what she wanted holding her. Now. Tomorrow. Forever. Her own skin burned, and she hurried her hands down to his forearms and on to his waist. Not a flicker of emotion crossed his face.

"No love handles," she said, pouting. Her hands ran easily around his waist above the towel. "But I guess a woman could find something else to hold on to."

"I haven't had any complaints," he murmured.

His detachment annoyed her, especially when she compared it to her own increasing heartbeat. Wasn't he affected at all by this? She wrapped her arms around his waist. "It hugs good," she said. His heart was racing too. She could hear it, she could feel it, but that face was still unmoving. She wasn't going to stop until he flinched.

Her hands separated and went up from his waist, along the muscles on the outside of his back. "Lats are well defined." A smile played on her lips as he started slightly. "Although a trifle sensitive." Several giggles escaped her lips, triggered by the fierce frown that seized his face. "Actually, strong but sensitive is a wonderful combination."

Dusty's heart was racing faster and faster. She felt almost light-headed, but couldn't—wouldn't—stop the explorations. Her hands floated up and across Pat's chest. The muscles were hard and beautifully defined under the thick, dark mat of hair. She wanted to feel those ripples and that power with her lips, but she pulled back, her mind trying to remain in command. Instead, she spread her hands open and let the whole of her palms and fingers delight in him and his strength.

"Chest is wonderful," she heard a breathy voice blurt out.

The look in his eyes darkened until it almost matched that of the rampaging Irish warrior of her dreams, the one whose body had been setting hers afire each night, and leaving her hungry and unsatisfied in the morning. Dusty decided it was time to regain control of herself and her hands. She drew them down to her sides.

"How about the legs?" he asked, his voice hoarse and slow.

"Legs?"

His eyes ate into her, twisting her stomach, squeezing the air from her lungs. "I checked your legs out. You should check mine out. It would only be fair."

Dusty looked down at the chiseled thighs visible below the towel. She wanted to touch them, she wanted to caress and feel, to explore and tease, not just with her hands, but with her lips, her legs. Her whole body was aching for his. It took all of Dusty's strength and the memory of Sister Ida Gannon, her high school principal, to control herself.

"We can save your legs for another day," she said.

Pat shook his head and stared at her for two-thirds of an eternity. "None of us is promised tomorrow."

She did not reply; she couldn't reply. This was just supposed to have been a game, a little bit of teasing revenge. She'd been dreaming of Pat, longing for his touch, but she hadn't really meant to come in here and seduce him. Had she? She would leave now, before things got out of hand.

Her legs had all the strength of melted ice and ignored her feeble requests for them to take her out into the hallway. She just stood there, desire burning her resolve into a pile of ashes.

Slowly Pat came to her and took her in his arms. Her hands, no longer quite so brave, went to rest on his neck and shoulders as his slid under her shirt to gently massage her back.

"Lats and deltoids beautiful," he murmured into her ear.

She leaned against him and let him nuzzle her

neck, his breath warming her, awakening her to need. With every gentle stroke of his lips on her skin, the fires raged hotter and hotter, threatening to engulf her. Her breath quickened and her eyes closed. His lips danced along her neck and around her ear, a slow, sensuous waltz that pushed her heartbeat into a pounding, primitive rhythm. His hands slid around to cup with possession the breasts that had been free under her shirt.

"Beautiful," he whispered.

Her whole being melted into him, moving without her permission, but with her approval. To be in his embrace was the heaven she'd dreamed of. Yet the Irish warrior of her fantasies was nothing compared to Pat. Pat was real; he was here. His lips left her skin and she cried out against the abandonment. "Pat. Pat."

But even as the whispered sighs were falling from her lips, Dusty could feel Pat's body coming to hers without the protective covering of his towel. His strength surrounded her with gentle possession. Their lips joined the passionate call, clinging in a wordless song of longing, a timeless melody of need and hunger and union.

Everything was going too fast. Dusty's world was spinning out of control and she feared they'd be thrown off. She tried to warn Pat of the dizzying heights she was soaring toward, but the heat of their hunger fused her words into a single groan and it slipped out unheeded. Her hands pushed her shirt away from her while Pat's hands tugged at her jeans. Their lips clung, parting briefly to allow her shirt to pass over her head, then joined again, fueling the fires between them to frightening intensity.

His body was rough against hers: strong, hard

muscles covered with a wiry matting of thick hair. The feel of it tantalized and delighted as her hands explored and pressed him closer. His chest and back seemed made of stone. Everywhere her hands roamed they slid across the rock-hardness of his muscles. The ferocious racing of his heart told of his hunger as her arching body told of hers.

He took her then, her wild Irish warrior. Carefully, he lowered her to the floor. Strength, power, and desire all fused into one trembling being, into one pulsating world as he entered her and overwhelmed her. Her legs wrapped around him, pulling him into her wonder, into her throbbing. His hands ignited and tempered, they cupped her breasts, singed her thighs, stoked the fire that was consuming her into a wild, uncontrollable blazing.

He was over her, in her, and all around her. He became her whole world and filled her being. She soared through the universe, bound only to Pat, clinging to him as her only source of reality until a violent explosion shook her and echoed through Pat, leaving them exhausted. She lay at his side breathing rapidly and hoarsely, still wrapped in his arms. A kaleidoscope of wonder danced through her head, longing and need, power and victory, tenderness and possession. Had she conquered him? Had he conquered her?

"Camilla."

The hoarse whisper coaxed her eyes open. She looked into his gaze and saw the whole world waiting for her there. The answer was yes.

"How was dinner?" Dusty whispered in Pat's ear.

"My compliments to the chef. Do you happen to remember his telephone number?"

Dusty pushed him down on his back on the living room rug and sprawled over his massive chest. "Don't be a smart aleck. Gino's is supposed to have some of the best pizza in the city."

"I could have fixed something," Pat said, dropping kisses as soft as rose petals along her neck.

"I didn't want your attention diverted."

His fingers had started massaging sunshine into her back. Dusty would have curled up and purred like a kitten except for the clouds flicking across the blue sky of his eyes.

"You're the boss," he murmured.

Sighing, Dusty raised herself up on her elbows. "Only in regard to your duties as butler," she said firmly. "This has nothing to do with a butler and his lady." She kissed him lightly on the lips. "It's strictly man and woman."

Pat stroked her cheek with the back of his hand. "So what do we do now, Camilla?"

The words rumbled in his chest, sending little tingles of excitement into her body. "What do we do with what?" she asked lazily.

"We had a working relationship. That's been complicated somewhat."

"We both have jobs," she said. "And we're also getting closer to each other. That's no different from thousands of other couples in this city, or the world, for that matter."

His face tightened into a scowl. "We don't just have jobs. In case you've forgotten, I work for you."

"The way you're always bossing me around, it's a wonder I don't forget."

"I'm sorry, I get a little out of control sometimes."

Dusty's laughter burst out. "I noticed that."

His Irish temper began to burn off his humility.

"Uh-oh," she said. "Paddy's getting mad."

"I'm not," he growled through clenched teeth, and pulled her down onto himself.

His lips hungrily seized hers, and Dusty could feel life stirring in all his muscles. Pat rolled her over on her back and took his place on top.

"We're going to keep our working relationship and our personal relationship strictly separate," he whispered in her ear.

"Are all the Irish so poetic?"

His lips came down on hers and subdued her grin, turning her body limp with pleasure.

Eight

"Well, there it is. Ain't it a beauty?"

Pat stared across the street at the old abandoned factory. "Looks big and solid. How is it structurally?"

Camilla's father shifted his ever-present cigar stub to the other side of his mouth before speaking. "It's got twelve-inch-thick brick walls. They don't build them like that anymore."

They crossed the street to get a closer look. The chain-link fence was sagging in spots, weeds had overgrown the old parking lots, and plywood covered many of the windows.

"Used to be a bicycle-assembly plant."

Pat grunted. "Managers moved the work overseas?"

The older man shrugged as he removed the cigar butt. "Overseas. Down south. Out of state. Same difference."

"Looks big enough," Pat said as they walked along the block.

"No doubt about it," Mr. Ross said. "The property goes all the way back to the tracks. You could wreck those old sheds over there and have parking to spare."

Pat merely nodded, but the excitement was building inside him. This might be just the spot. It looked so bad on the outside that he and his partners might get it for a song, leaving them enough capital to do the renovations.

"You're within walking distance of a hundred and fifty thousand people with a lot of money to spend," Mr. Ross pointed out. "And near enough to the expressways and public transportation to tap another three hundred thousand. Want to see the inside?" Mr. Ross led him to a remote corner of the property, lifted a side of the fence, and they slipped in.

Pat stared up at the building—the broken, gaping windows, the graffiti on the walls, and the air of hopelessness. The place reminded him of that factory his mother had been working in when he'd left home, the one his money had been too late to save her from. In a way, it was fitting that such a place should give him the chance to live, the chance for happiness. He had vowed back then that he'd never marry until he could support a wife and family completely, without a dime from anyone else. Maybe this building was his ticket to doing just that.

And it couldn't come too soon for him; he wasn't keen on this new arrangement with Camilla at all. It wasn't right, no matter how perfectly her body fit along his. He should be strong enough to remember his duties; he should be strong enough to remember he wasn't in a position to take care of her, not in the protective, sheltering ways a real man takes care of his woman. But all he could remember when he was near her was his hunger as a man and her warmth as a woman.

Maybe he was foolish, too old-fashioned in his thinking. He'd had other women before, ones he'd held and kissed knowing they had no future together, but never had they aroused such feelings of guilt. These were modern times. He should just relax and learn to enjoy himself. No one was asking him if his intentions were honorable; no one cared. Long-term commitments were outdated.

They rounded the corner of the building and found about six or eight people gathered around a fire. A steel bucket was hanging over it, but the people were staring at the two strangers.

"Don't mind us," Pat said. "Me and my friend are just looking around."

He and Mr. Ross passed and made their way into the building. "The maid's been sick the past two days," a voice croaked after them. "So the place is a bit untidy." Wheezes that must have been laughter followed.

Once they were inside, Pat concentrated on the building, pushing Camilla from his mind. The place looked well built, though his architect partner would be the one to decide that. It certainly could contain the multi levels they wanted, and stores of varying sizes.

"It's great," Pat said simply.

They left the same way they had come and walked the mile or so east to Camilla's house. "Who's in this group of yours?" Mr. Ross asked. "Any need for an old guy with construction background and some money to invest?"

"You want in?" Pat asked.

"Sure." Dusty Senior shrugged. "Retirement's getting dull, and I'd like to see some of these old places reborn. Maybe Camilla could even give us a hand."

No, she couldn't. Not in his book. "We'll have to look at a lot of alternatives."

"She is a commercial real estate agent, you know," her father pressed.

She was also his boss and his lover. That modern he couldn't be; he couldn't let her do everything for him. "I know what she does for a living," Pat snapped. "But this is my affair and I'll handle it, thank you."

Silence surrounded them the rest of the way, like the damp, penetrating fogs of Liverpool. Pat shoved his hands into his pockets and strode along, feeling uncomfortable and churlish. There hadn't been any reason to snap at Camilla's father except Pat's own dislike of the situation.

Being her butler and her lover was enough to churn up all sorts of doubts and fears as to who he was, as to what kind of man resided in his body. It caused all the past generations of Mahoneys to hover over him, frowning with disapproval while exhorting him to be a man. He didn't need to lean on her for anything else.

"Care for lunch?" he asked Mr. Ross when their steps slowed outside Camilla's house. "I bought a six-pack of Beck's."

The older man shrugged. "I've already lived a long life," he said. "I'll give it a try."

"How the hell is my lunch going to kill you?"

"I have high standards. My system goes into shock if they're not met."

Silence shouldered its way between them again as

they went upstairs, but it became more companionable once they each had a beer next to them. Pat made submarine sandwiches: a bed of shredded lettuce laid out on two fresh loaves of French bread and piled high with meats and cheeses.

"Do you want mayonnaise or Thousand Island?" Pat asked.

Mr. Ross covered his face with his hands and silently shook his head.

"Okay," Pat muttered. He put Italian dressing on both sandwiches and carried them to the table.

"Not bad for an Irishman," Mr. Ross said after the first bite.

"It's hard to tell what you really like," Pat grunted. "You're so effusive in your praise of everything."

They ate most of their sandwiches without talking until Mr. Ross broke the silence. "Camilla seems a lot happier lately. You must be good for her."

Pat stopped, a piece of sandwich in his mouth. Fathers were not supposed to approve of their daughter's butlers slipping into more intimate roles. His eyes tried to see into the other man's mind.

Dusty Senior was eating away, seemingly unconcerned. After another bite he went on. "She seemed to have a good time at the soccer game Friday night. Laughed a lot and really relaxed. Been a long time since I've seen her so carefree."

Pat slowly completed his bite. "She works hard," he said. "Doesn't relax as much as she ought to."

His mind took him back to the previous Sunday, when they had loafed around the apartment the whole day. A miserable rain had kept them indoors, but their mood had been anything but depressed. Then yesterday when she'd come home from work he'd had a special dinner waiting. Special because it had kept so nicely while they got reacquainted after being separated for eight long hours. He hadn't had any problems with their relationship then. Why was he having second thoughts now?

Mr. Ross nodded his head. "She was always intense about everything she did."

Pat drank his beer with unusual concentration until his butlering frame of mind was firmly back in place. "I think that burglary a few months back unsettled her. She's more relaxed having someone else around the apartment."

If her father had other theories, he gave no sign, and Camilla wasn't brought back into the conversation until he was leaving. "Sorry about trying to push Camilla into your deal," Mr. Ross said. "I just hated to think of her losing on the commission."

"Everything's a little tenuous right now," Pat replied. "I'm sure we'd all be glad to have your expertise, but I'd hate to see Camilla waste her time at this stage."

Dusty Senior nodded and waved his good-bye, leaving Pat staring at the closed door a long time before he went to his quarters. He would relax and enjoy things and stop all his worrying. What was that phrase? Go with the flow? That's what he would do from now on.

"I'm home," Dusty called out but barely took time to look at the mail. Wednesday never brought anything interesting anyway. Her eyes flicked over the living room. It was perfectly neat. Empty.

"Hi." Pat appeared down the hall and she read the welcome in his eyes as well as heard it in his voice.

"Hi yourself."

He took her coat and briefcase, then took her in his arms. The worries of the day were evicted by his kisses, sweet and soft and warm. She had given him title to her heart, happily and without reservation.

"So how was your day?" he asked, allowing her to remain a tenant in his arms.

"Busy." She pulled his head down to hers again for a repeat of those soft, gentle touches that rehabilitated her soul. "Lonesome." Her mouth sought his once more, drinking the peace and serenity of his strength. The world began to unwind, and she relaxed against his chest.

"You're home early," he said, the words rumbling beneath her ear.

A willful finger crept up, sliding in between the buttons of his shirt to feel the roughness of his skin. His hand closed around the finger and brought it up to his mouth. A single kiss calmed the finger's mischievousness, but started a frenzy deep within her.

"Is that a problem?" The finger traced his lips until it was captured once again.

"Dinner won't be ready for hours."

Her eyes caught the gleam in his. "Hours?"

"Well, at least an hour and a half."

"I see." Her other hand opened his top button, then the next. "I suppose I could go back to work."

His hand undid the belt at her waist. "I suppose you could."

Another button opened, and then the last two. Her hand slid across his hairy chest. "It would be a good chance to get caught up on some of my paperwork."

The zipper on the front of her dress was tugged down, a little train racing down the track. "Yes, it would."

"I've never minded busy work." She loosened his belt.

He pushed her dress from her shoulders. "I've always admired that about you."

"Oh?"

He swept her up into his arms. "Your ability to keep your hands busy."

"Funny you should mention my hands." One arm went around his neck, the other hand ran through his hair. "They have this notion of how they'd like to keep busy right now. . . ."

"What did they do wrong this time?" Dusty asked. The remains of their Mexican dinner lay on the low table before them as she and Pat watched a Sunday-evening soccer game on television.

"He used his hands. I told you, only the goalie can touch the ball with his hands."

"That seems like a stupid rule. How can you play without your hands?"

"It's not that hard. Come on." He pulled her to her feet and pushed their dinner table aside, then tossed a throw pillow onto the floor. "There, that'll be the soccer ball. See, there's lots you can do with your feet."

He proceeded to show off, tapping it this way and that, picking it up with his foot and tossing it into the air. When it came back down to earth she plunked her foot down on top of it.

"Hey, you aren't supposed to step on the ball," he cried.

She just smiled. "I'm not using my hands."

He put his arms around her and lifted her off the pillow.

"No fair!" she protested. "Or can't you win without cheating?"

His eyes glittered. "Oh-ho, is this a challenge to the Mahoney honor?" He looked around him and grabbed up two magazines, putting them on the floor at opposite ends of the room. "That's my goal, this one is yours. Whoever gets the pillow on their goal first wins."

"No hands?"

"No hands."

Pat called out "Go!" and threw his concentration to the pillow/ball, trying to push it along the floor with his feet. Dusty was more interested in him. She pressed her body, hands carefully behind her back, against him. Her breasts rubbed against his chest; her thigh pressed into him.

"Hey!" he cried out.

"I'm not using my hands," she said sweetly.

It was easy, and much more fun, to keep her eyes on him rather than on the silly pillow. Her legs teased him, her lips invited, and her eyes challenged. The sway of her hips met the rock of his body.

"I see we've changed the object of the game," he murmured, his eyes darkening.

While she was pressed against him his lips came down on her neck, tickled her ear, and breathed fire into her blood. The noise of cheering came from the television.

"Seems like everybody likes the new game," she said.

"It has a nice feel to it."

Their lips found each other's and drank hungrily; their mouths crushed together as their bodies had done. But soon it wasn't enough. Her hands crept out to touch him. Her arms went around him.

"Foul," he whispered. "Send her to the penalty box."

His hands forgot the rules, too, sweeping over her back, drawing her body ever nearer.

"Two minutes?" she asked.

"For such a major infraction? Ten minutes wouldn't be enough. An hour at least. Maybe even the whole night."

"You're late," was Pat's greeting.

She blew a kiss at his fierce scowl and dropped her textbooks into the nearest chair. "Only because I was following all your admonitions. I parked in a well-lighted spot. I waited for someone to walk with me to the parking lot, and I drove only on busy streets."

His scowl softened. "I don't like your being out late by yourself. Maybe I should start picking you up from school."

"Pat, that's really not necessary."

"I'm not so sure of that." He took her coat and hung it up. "Have you eaten?"

She held her hand up like a witness called to testify. "A full meal: salad, green beans, and broiled fish." She grinned. "Not nearly as good as yours."

"But kept you from being hungry."

"Oh, I wouldn't say that."

His eyes answered her gleam, his mouth echoed her laughter. "I see." He bolted the outside door and walked slowly into the living room to turn off a lamp. "So you're still hungry, are you?"

"Starving."

Light trickled toward them from the hallway. He put his arms gently around her. "I could make you a salad," he suggested. "Sweet, tender Boston lettuce.

Kissed by the sun and caressed with a vinaigrette dressing, made as only I can make it." His lips explained the technique; his hands gave a demonstration.

"Feels delicious, but not quite what I had in mind."

His hands and lips stilled into thoughtfulness for a moment, then he pulled her blouse from the waistband of her skirt, moving his hands under it. "How about some soup? Nice and hot and steaming to warm up any hidden corners that might be cold?"

"I'm not cold." She snuggled up close to him, her own hands under his shirt. "In fact, I'm rather warm. Hot, even."

"Baked Alaska then. Sweet and rich and creamy. As refreshing as a stolen night of love."

"Sounds fattening."

His hands loosened her bra and crept around her body to her breasts. His touch felt cool to her heated skin.

"What will we do to satisfy you?" he murmured into her hair.

"Are you all out of suggestions?" Her voice was breathless and hoarse.

"I'll find something," he promised.

The bed was empty, cold, and lonely. Dusty rolled over to look the other way, but the emptiness could still be felt. It wasn't just the bed; it filled the whole room. Knowing sleep would never come back, she got out of bed. Her robe lay by itself on the chair, a nagging reminder that neither she nor it had lain alone last night. She pulled it around her shoulders and went into the kitchen. Pat was dressed in white shirt, dark pants, and his butlering face.

"Morning."

He turned when she spoke and nodded. "Morning, ma'am." If any warmth seeped into his face, she saw no sign of it. "Would you like a cup of coffee while you dress?"

"Thanks." She leaned wearily against the refrigerator while he poured the coffee and added just the right touch of milk. This couldn't be the same man who had surrounded her with tenderness last night, whose hands had stormed her senses and conquered her soul. What did he do? Take a butler pill each morning with his vitamins?

He handed her the cup, careful not to let their hands brush, then went back to beating the eggs or whatever task he was so intent on.

"There's no need for you to get up so early on Saturdays," she pointed out. She knew he was bothered by the inequality of their positions, but wasn't sure how to convince him it didn't matter. If their shared passion couldn't tell him that, what good were mere words?

He did not turn. "I need to get your breakfast started."

"How long does it take to scramble a couple of eggs? I'd rather wake up with you still next to me."

He abandoned his egg beating and began to empty the dishwasher. Glasses, cups, plates, and bowls were all lined up with precision on the counter. "This is my job and I have to do it the way I feel best."

"Well, I feel best—"

He ignored her attempt at teasing. "Taking care of the house and the meals is my responsibility. It's what you pay me for."

Why was he always bringing that up? What was that stubborn Irish conscience of his telling him to do? She wished there were a way to turn it off, or lock it up in a safety deposit box down at the bank. It was his damn conscience that was feeding him those but-lering pills, and she was getting tired of the seesaw ride. "I'm going to take a shower before I eat," she said, and took her coffee back to her room.

Mornings weren't their best time. Pat awoke with the festering need to remind her of their roles, while she woke with a hunger for love.

Breakfast had become a formal meal. Every day something new was added: dining-room location, good china, linen napkins and a tablecloth. Yester-day it had been a bell to summon him with. She had thrown it at him, refusing it and the whole meal. By the time she got home from work the need to butler appeared to have been wrung from his system, but only to be reborn the next morning.

She didn't care if she paid his salary, she told the shower door. It made no difference to her feelings for him. Their situation was no different from that of many couples, except that it was more usual for the man to share his salary with the woman. Still, that was no reason for Pat's moods. Maybe they just needed a diversion.

Showered, dressed, and armed with a determina-tion to slay the butler-beast that had devoured her Pat, she went back into the kitchen. "I think I'd like to get out of town for the weekend."

He busied himself with the final preparations of her breakfast, perfectly aligning the pan on the stove, straightening the strips of bacon. Had he counted the coffee beans? "Very good, madam. I'm sure you'll enjoy the change."

She stuck out her tongue at his straight, stubborn back, then went into the dining room to retrieve her place setting. "I meant for us both to go," she told him upon her return.

He frowned at the dishes she'd put on the kitchen table. "If that's what madam wishes."

"Madam doesn't wish. I do." She sat down heavily and crossed her arms. "And that damn little bow tie stays home." If only she could order his conscience to do the same.

Nine

Pat's mood lightened as they left the city, like fog melted by the sun. By the time they were racing along the highway toward historic Galena, he was smiling. Dusty knew it had been the right decision to go. Away from the house they'd be more relaxed, and she could get him to see how things had changed. Sure, he was still technically her butler, but they were a modern couple. She forgot his job most of the time, and so could he.

"If you get tired, I'll take my turn at driving," she offered.

Pat smiled. "I'll let you drive whenever we get in a city. That's where you Americans give me problems with your annoying habit of driving on the wrong side of the road."

She frowned. "As I remember, Europe drives on the same side of the road as we do. England is the only country that drives on the left side."

"Not so. England, Japan, Jamaica, and other commonwealth nations all do."

"Canada doesn't."

He shrugged. "There are always a few oddballs."

"The oddballs are the majority."

"But you agree they are the oddballs."

Dusty let him think he had won the argument; she was just glad to have his teasing back. She stared out of the window at the farms lining the Northwest Tollway in this part of Illinois, relieved that he had stopped deferring to her constantly. His smile had returned to warm and caring; his eyes spoke of desire, not duty. Off in the distance she saw colts prancing about on stiff legs. This year spring had marked the beginning of life not just for newborn animals, but for her too.

"I guess winter has a purpose after all," she said, pushing aside the silence. "It makes spring so wonderful. I almost feel sorry for those places that have no seasons."

"The whole world has a cycle of seasons," he pointed out. "Warm and cold. Wet and dry. Light and dark."

"I hadn't thought of that."

"Cycles are a fixed part of our world," he went on. "Birth and death. Beginning and end. They're immutable."

Dusty twisted her lips and looked out the window. Next he'd be saying employer and employee and they'd be back where they started from. They didn't need a trip to Galena to do that.

The road plunged onward through the farm communities of northern Illinois. They were like little pieces of another time, a different world from the city. She and Pat were different too. Just lovers, that was all. No titles of butler or lady of the house to bind them to uncomfortable roles.

"Ah, we're approaching the home of Tuddy Baker," he said suddenly.

She glanced at him, surprised. "You have friends in Freeport?"

His laugh touched her even though his eyes stayed on the road. "Freeport got its name from Old Tuddy, or actually from his wife. His real name was William, but the Indians called him Tuddy because he stuttered."

"Is this for real?" He was so good at spinning yarns, she didn't know whether to believe him or not.

"Of course," he said. "Tuddy Baker was an extremely hospitable man whose door was always open any time of the day or night. This so aggravated Mrs. Baker that she accused her husband of operating a free port."

"How'd you learn that?" Dusty asked.

"I read."

"I read too."

He shook his head as if in dismissal. "Real estate ads, textbooks, business magazines. I read for the pleasure of learning new things."

Dusty kicked off her shoes and brought her knees up under her chin as she silently watched the road. She'd like to say she read for pleasure, too, but outside of her Irish warrior book, she hadn't had time for anything other than necessities. She was busy. Too busy?

"When I first came to Chicago I got hooked on Illinois history," he said. "But I guess that can be said of each place I've lived. I like the sense of being a part of things, of treasuring what went before me and hoping those after me will do the same."

She had barely noticed the places she'd been except to decide how to get someplace better. An uneasy feeling that she might have been missing good things settled on her.

Galena 48 miles, the sign announced, but some of the excitement of the trip had flown. It wasn't Pat's doing; it was her own. She was beginning to see how narrow her life had been. Narrow and stuffy.

Pat glanced at her and must have read her change of mood. "Did you know Galena was originally called Fever River?"

"A realtor must have fixed that in a hurry," Dusty remarked.

Their laughter drove the cobwebs of gloom away from her. They drove the rest of the way in silence because the road's twists and turns required Pat's full attention. Dusty drank in vistas of rolling hills and sweeping valleys that no camera or canvas could capture. A god with a desire for variety had diverted the glaciers away from this corner of Illinois. The rest of the Midwest had all the varied terrain of a shopping center parking lot, but this area was special—a place of unique beauty, she realized suddenly. A treasure for her and Pat to share.

About an hour later they plunged into the valley that cupped the town of Galena.

"Any special hotel you have in mind?" Pat asked.

"No," she admitted. "Let's find something small and romantic."

They drove the streets lined with red-brick buildings clinging to the steep hillsides until they found a rambling two-story house with a turret. A small sign announced the availability of bed and board.

A tall lady with an old-fashioned pageboy haircut answered their knock. Black dye hid all her gray hairs just as hard green eyes hid all traces of softness and pleasantness in her face.

"Good morning, madam," Pat boomed. "Would you be having room in your heart and home for two travelers weary from the dirt and toil of the city?"

Before Dusty could generate a groan the woman's face broke into a smile, transformed before Dusty's eyes. "You're a little early in the season and the day. If you could give me some time, I can have a real nice room fixed up for you and your lady."

"That would be wonderful," Pat replied with a broad smile. "With your permission, we'll be putting our auto in your drive and then taking a stroll down to the green for a spot of coffee and sweetness."

"Sure." Still trying to adjust to her newfound pleasantness, the woman looked at Dusty for the first time. "I'll put you and your fella in that corner room up there," she said, pointing to a window on the second floor. "It's big and sunny with a private bath and queen-size bed."

"That'll be fine."

"I used to say mister and missus," the innkeeper said, following them down the porch steps. "Can't really do that anymore. There's no way of knowing."

Dusty had to work to keep her smile straight. "That's true."

"Don't matter to me none." The woman stopped on the bottom step. "Things are better the way they are now. I don't like to mess in other people's affairs, and I don't like them messing in mine."

"We're actually horses of a completely different color," Pat said, slipping his arm around Dusty's shoulders. "I'm her butler."

The woman just laughed heartily, and a high, cackling sound that didn't match the woman's husky build filled the silent air. "Don't matter none." She turned to climb the steps. "Give me an hour," she called back.

A small part of Dusty's mind heard the woman, but the rest of her was watching Pat. Why had he said that? His job had been the fly in their ointment all along, and she didn't want any buzzings to disturb their perfect weekend. His smile seemed unchanged, though, and the slight humming under his breath was relaxed. She let a sigh escape her as she took his arm. Maybe it didn't really bother him as much as she thought.

The day passed in a delightful haze. They hiked through the wild countryside and poked amid the dusty treasures of local antique shops. Pat seemed to melt the hearts of everyone they met, so the town seemed like home, especially during their dinner when they became fast friends of not only their waitress, but the owner of the restaurant and the chef, a little Italian man.

"It's the fatal Mahoney charm," Pat explained as they walked back to the boardinghouse.

"Oh, is it?"

"Aye." He lapsed into his brogue. "Why, you ought to know, having been smitten by it yourself."

"Oh, have I?" She ran away from him, laughing from the sheer joy of spring, from the happiness of being alive, of being with Pat. How had she existed before she met him? What purpose had there been for laughter? For smiles? For spring flowers and gentle breezes?

Pat caught up with her easily, and swung her up in

his arms. "There's no escaping," he said. "Once smitten, you'll always be mine."

She laughed and clung to him with her lips as well as her arms. The fire smoldering in her all day flared up. It was so true; she would always be his. She loved him.

All her life she'd been waiting—a spectator, not a player, in life. Now her reason for living was here, opening doors and windows and showing her the wonders that love held. She blindly followed his lead; fear was a thing for the future or the past. It had no place in her present. There was room only for Pat.

He put her down and they walked hand in hand through the shadows of the budding oak trees. The earth smelled new and fresh. Alive. Her cotton skirt and blouse moved with her rhythm and the sway of the evening's breeze.

"You look especially"—he hesitated a long moment—"appealing."

Appealing? The soft tenderness in his voice made her feel vibrant and full of life. Sexy. She dropped Pat's hand and put her arm around his waist, pulling him against herself. His free arm went around her shoulders and hugged her to him. Then he stopped, his lips drinking of hers. His thirst was obvious.

"Am I really appealing?" The notion delighted her.

"You're a damn temptress," he growled hoarsely. "A seductive siren who's destroyed all my best intentions."

They walked on in silence. The sun was sinking down behind the hills, its rays falling into the Mississippi River to catch a ride to New Orleans.

They climbed up the wooden steps to the boardinghouse. A swing hung from the porch ceiling, moving with the wind or memories of past couples. "Want to sit out here awhile?" Pat asked.

"No!" Dusty was surprised by the vehemence of her body's callings.

He stepped back from her and bowed formally. "Your slave awaits your command, milady."

She stared into his laughing eyes for a moment, bewilderment pulling at her. Were her fantasies so obvious? Recklessness seized her. "Your lady bids you go upstairs."

"Oh, no," Pat burst out in a howl. He put his hands to his face. "Not again. I can't take any more."

Embarrassment melted her imperious stance. "Pat." She laughed. "Stop that. Someone will hear you."

"I pray to God that someone will," he exclaimed. "How else will I be rescued from your voracious hunger? Oh, mercy," he called out, gasping between gales of laughter as she dragged him inside. "Please, have mercy."

"Never," she cried out. He was ridiculously easy to drag along.

"Aren't you ashamed of your appetites?" he asked. "Of abusing your poor servant this way?"

They had reached their room by that time and Pat closed the door, his eyes alight with his need for her, his smile as wide as his outstretched arms. Her own smile had been lost somewhere on the stairs amid his joking.

His arms dropped and his smile dimmed. "Camilla? What's the matter?"

"Nothing." She picked up a section of the newspaper from the pile on the dresser, kicked off her shoes, and sat down in the middle of the bed to read. To pretend to read. Were there really words on these pages?

Pat's constant reminders that she was his employer hurt. He wasn't going to bed with her to keep his job, but was he doing it out of love? He'd never mentioned it, and she wouldn't exactly say he suffered from shyness.

"You're mad at me, aren't you?"

"I'm reading the paper right now."

Dusty forced herself to focus on the page in front of her. Damn. It was the living arts section of some paper from Dubuque. She wanted to throw it aside, but Pat was standing right there. If she wanted another section of the paper, she'd have to reach around him.

"I was only joking," he said. "Come on, Camilla. Humor is the spice that makes life palatable."

"I hadn't realized how distasteful life was for you," she said. "It must be just awful to be subjected to the overbearing advances of a lustful employer." Besides, she didn't consider her love a joke. The poor lighting in the room was causing the page to blur. She squinted to bring it back in focus.

"It's a burden I try to bear bravely and without complaint."

"I'm not in the mood for any more of your sophomoric humor."

"I never was a sophomore."

"Don't worry about it, you're eminently qualified."

He sat down behind her, looking over her shoulder at the paper, his breath gently moving her hair, his lips nibbling at her neck. She wouldn't give in to the need to lie back against him. She wouldn't move her hand to cover the one so close to hers.

Silence crept into the room, wrapping itself around her and stealing her oxygen. Her breathing rasped annoyingly in her ears. The only thing louder was the ticking of the clock on the mantel.

Dusty couldn't stand it anymore. "Are you done with this page?" she said through clenched teeth even though she hadn't read a word of it.

"Sure are some interesting articles, aren't there? I think my favorite's the one about the garden club meeting."

"They were all fascinating," she said carefully.

"True," he admitted.

She felt him stirring behind her. She didn't want him to leave. She wanted him to calm all the fears burning inside her, but she wouldn't ask him to. She had some pride left.

There was a warm breath on her ankle and then a light kiss. He had only turned toward her feet. "I'm sorry," he murmured.

Dusty renewed her concentration. She found a word on the page that she knew. She just couldn't remember what it was.

The warm breath traveled up to the middle of her calf. Another kiss. "I'm very sorry."

She shook the paper, trying to shake the letters—the words—into some sensible order. "No, you're not. You're just trying to be funny again."

"Laughter is life's mask for a cry of pain."

"You're very good at twisting words around for your own purpose."

A light ticklish sensation went across her right knee. "This knee has a beautiful smile," Pat said.

She scowled at the paper. Nothing of hers was smiling.

The sensation moved to her left knee. "So does this one."

"Stop it." The sharp order was for her own body as well as his fingers. It was ignored by all.

"I'm really very, very sorry," he said. A gentle kiss floated down onto her thigh. The heavy cotton of her skirt did nothing to shield her from the severity of the blow.

Why did he have such power over her? Why did her heart stop at the sight of him and race at his touch? She no longer owned herself. He teased her about being her slave, but in reality she was his. Whatever he wanted was fine, she needed him so. She had no will left, no pride.

He turned her and gently pushed her back against the bedspread. Then his lips found hers.

"I hate you," she lied, forcing the words out quickly before his mouth smothered hers again.

He pulled back, smiling. "The poets say that hate and love are separated by a line as thin as a moment."

Dusty surrendered herself unconditionally to that moment.

The turrets on the last building slipped behind the hills and even Dusty's longing couldn't keep them in sight. She turned around with a sigh and stared out ahead of them.

"It was a nice weekend," she said. Walking together, sleeping together, waking together.

"Yes, it was." His words agreed with her, but his face reflected the gloom of the darkening sky as night approached.

She frowned and stared out her window. He was probably sorry to see the wonderful weekend end, that was all. She mustn't let herself get all depressed because they were going back. Their magic would continue. The place didn't matter, just the fact that they were together. Chicago could nurture their love as well as Galena.

"Looks like we're in for some rain." She kept her voice light and chatty. "We were lucky the weather stayed so nice. April in northern Illinois isn't always the most stable of months, weatherwise."

"Must have been those orders I left with the weather gods," Pat joked.

His voice was strained, the teasing sounding forced, but she loved him all the more for his effort to keep her spirits up. She rested her head on his shoulder and let her eyes slip closed. "Oh, so I owe the beauty of the weekend to you?"

"That you do."

She smiled, unable to dispute his claim. She did owe him for the weekend, in more ways than one. Quite literally she owed him for the meals and their room at the boardinghouse. People assumed the man would pay, and always presented Pat with the bill, but they were a modern couple, beyond the need for such role-playing. Rather than make a fuss over it, she'd just reimburse him once they got home. Although she recalled that she had never paid him back for the bicycles they'd rented. Oh, well. More important was the deep, contented happiness he'd brought to her life. There was no way she could ever repay him for that, though she'd be happy to spend the rest of her life trying.

Ten

"Hot dog," Camilla exclaimed. "There's a parking place right in front."

Pat watched her maneuver the car into the narrow confines of the space. He hated parallel parking, but as usual Camilla did it well. She did everything well. He tried to push away the fog of melancholia threatening to engulf him, but it wouldn't budge. The weekend had been too good, too perfect. For thirty-two hours he had taken care of Camilla, pretended that he could, but now the dream was over.

Camilla turned the motor off and leaned back with a sigh. "It was a wonderful weekend, but it's nice to be home."

"I imagine it is," Pat said, and ignored her quizzical look as he got out of the car. This ought to be their home, but it wasn't. It wasn't his. He hadn't had a home for about twenty years now, and his last one, that grimy three-room flat he'd left at fourteen, wasn't anything to remember fondly.

He slammed the door solidly and went around to the trunk. He had left home for fame and fortune. He'd had a little fame, not as much fortune. Still, he hadn't done badly for himself. Now it was just a matter of time before he'd be able to have a home of his own.

"Are you mad about something?" Camilla asked, following him.

"No, of course not."

"I'm glad to hear that," she said. "I presume you slammed the door just to flex your muscles."

"I didn't slam the door," Pat said as evenly as he could. "That door just needs a solid push to stay closed." He opened the trunk and reached in quickly, grabbing all four valises. He put the smaller ones under each arm and held the larger in his hands.

"I can carry some," Camilla protested.

"This is my job." Time to get back to reality.

He hurried toward the front door. Camilla was probably making faces at his back, but that kind of childish nonsense was her prerogative. After all, she held the purse strings for the time being.

Suddenly he spun around, feeling more than hearing Camilla's squeaky gasp. She was looking to her left, where three husky boys, wearing gang colors, had stepped from between the buildings onto the dark street. They were walking toward them.

"Hey, Paddy," the taller one called out. "How ya doin'?"

"Good evening, gentlemen," Pat said with a nod.

"Evenin', ma'am," the spokesman said, tipping his beret to Camilla. The other two nodded and touched two fingers to the tips of their berets.

"Hello," she said. Her voice was a trifle higher than normal.

"Like later, Paddy," the leader called back over his shoulder.

"By later I presume you mean tomorrow night," Pat said firmly. "Eight o'clock sharp. St. Sebastian's gym."

Camilla stared after them as the boys disappeared into the darkness. "Friends of yours?" she asked.

"We're working on it." He had been working with the neighborhood association almost from the first days he had moved in, but there hadn't been any reason to tell Camilla about it. It wasn't taking that much of his time and wasn't any of her business anyway. After all, the colonies had banned slavery long ago. She couldn't, and didn't, own him.

They went up to the apartment in silence. Pat dropped his battered valise at the doorway to his quarters, and carried Camilla's bags on into her bedroom. He opened them and began unpacking, putting dirty clothes into a neat pile, laying the shoes in a straight row on the floor, and taking her beauty appliances into the bathroom.

Camilla came in. "I can do that."

"It's my job."

"I was going to do it later," she said. "Let's just relax. Maybe there's a good movie on TV or maybe even a bad movie. I don't care. I just want to relax. Together."

He didn't want to relax with her. He wasn't in the mood for relaxing. That was what they had done all weekend; he was back at work now. "My duties as a butler are to tidy up after you. They do not include watching the telly and relaxing."

"What's wrong with you tonight?"

Pat shook his head sadly as he put her shoes into the closet. "What's this country coming to? I'm just trying to do my job and there's something wrong with me."

"Boy, you're in rare form. You must have taken a grumpy pill and a martyr pill along with your butler pill." She threw herself onto the bed, took her shoes off, and tossed them into the corner. He moved to pick them up. "Leave them there," she shouted.

"It's my job to—"

"I don't want to be tidy," she cried. She threw her pillows to opposite sides of the room, shoved her covers into a disheveled pile on top of the bed, and plopped herself back down on the mess. "There, now I'm comfortable."

"As you wish, madam," he said with a slight bow.

"Don't give me that butler bull, Paddy me love. I remember a few times when you were able to put aside your all-consuming interest in tidiness."

His face burned, the flames fueled by feelings he had yet to examine, reasons he preferred not to look at. "I'd better wash these things," he said, gathering up the pile from the floor.

"Pat!"

So she was finally ordering him around like the servant he was. He glared at her, but her eyes had changed. Where there had been lightning, dark clouds lingered, ready to release a downpour. The flames of his anger were quickly doused.

"Excuse me, madam." He stalked off to the basement laundry room with the pile of clothes and shoved a load into the washer.

"Damn!" He slammed the washer shut and started its cycle, cursing his ancestors as he pounded the top

of the washer for emphasis. "Damn! Damn! Damn!"
He had fallen in love with Camilla.

His ancestors fled from his anger, leaving the echoes of their nagging behind. Take her. Conquer her. That had been their advice that Saturday morning. The pride of the Mahoneys was at stake, they had claimed. And now they were berating him for having been a fool and falling into her trap.

The long drive home had tired his eyes, and Pat rubbed them now to alleviate the burning sensation. Which was he? Fool or ravisher? The answer came in the form of a vision, a dainty little lady with blue eyes ready to overflow in a torrent of tears.

A man—a real man—didn't just take. He gave, without counting, without caring the cost. He protected. He provided for. And if he couldn't do that properly, then he didn't take. Not even a lady's smile.

The washing machine filled with water and settled into its churning action. Pat eased himself down on the basement floor and stared at the light-green concrete walls. What a useless excuse for a man he was! He couldn't afford to take care of the lady and yet he took from her.

When she'd first opened her door to him and he saw what a beautiful vision she was, he should have run. But no, not him. All he'd been thinking of was the job. So what if she had fainted soon after he walked in? There had been no reason for him to stay once he knew she was all right.

There was no justification for his actions. He had wanted the job. It was room and board, a few dollars, and a lot of time for himself. Time to chase his dream, his dream to be a bigshot.

No, it was worse than that. It wasn't just ambition that had prompted him to take the job. Even then he had sensed that Camilla was special. And knowing that he had nothing yet to offer her but dreams, he had stayed to taste her love. Because he couldn't tear himself away.

The weekend was as things could have been, how they ought to be, but now was as they were. The truth was sitting here, staring him in the eye, daring him to see it. He loved her, yet he was living off her bounty. He was a bounder, a cad.

The silence brought Pat up alert. Here he was mooning about and feeling sorry for himself and Camilla's clothes were all done. He resolutely pushed himself up and transferred the clothes to the dryer.

"That's enough self-pity, boyo," he told himself as he slammed the dryer shut. "You've made a mistake, but it's not too late to be a man again."

Dusty laid Pat's electric razor, comb, and brush on the ledge next to the sink. It was obvious from the arrangement of his medicine cabinet that he had a specific place for everything, so she'd better let him put his things away. She turned and left his bathroom, sad that she didn't know him better. From now on she was going to get involved in every nook and cranny of his life.

She took his shirts out of the suitcase and noticed a slip of paper stuffed into the pocket of one. It was the receipt for their room. She took a pencil off his nightstand and sat down on the bed. She owed him for more than just the room. Tolls, their meals, bicycle rentals. She paused. And gas. Even though she had a credit card, Pat had insisted on paying cash.

"What are you doing?"

Engrossed in her numbers, Dusty didn't hear Pat

come into the room and she jumped half out of her skin.

"You frightened me." She laughed.

"I'm sorry." His face was stern and solemn. "But what are you doing?"

"I was just returning a favor," she said, waving her hand to indicate the items and suitcase on the bed. "You put my stuff away and I was putting your stuff away."

"I wasn't doing you any favors," he reminded her. "It's my job, and you pay me for it."

A coldness touched her heart and stopped her breath for a moment. He must have taken a double-strength butler pill or maybe he had a new timed-release version.

"I'm sorry to be such a bother." The words had an icy edge to them. Dusty let a small sigh escape, then she took a deep breath and forced a smile to her lips, hoping to minimize the damage. "I was just trying to figure out how much I owe you," she said, nodding to the receipt in her hand.

His face grew even more stern, and she felt a sinking feeling in her stomach.

"You don't owe me anything."

"The trip was my idea," she insisted. "And I pay my own way. I'm not a leech."

"And I am?"

Fear kicked her stomach sharply and drove all the air from her lungs. She had never seen stone melt, but the stony glare of Pat's eyes melted into pain. She had hurt him. "I'm sorry. I didn't mean it that way," she pleaded. "It's just that I always pay and—"

"I know you always pay," he snapped at her. "Don't you think I'm aware of that? Don't you think I have any damn feelings? I am a man, you know."

She came forward and touched his arm. "I have never doubted that," she said almost in a whisper.

He pulled away from her. "I mean a real man, Camilla. A man of honor, not a gigolo."

His anger swirled around them like feathers let loose in the wind. She couldn't see what was at the heart of it, what was causing his distress. She had to defuse his anger. She had to push it away from them and clear the air.

"Okay," she said. "You can pay for the trip. It's not that big a deal. It doesn't matter."

The words hung in the air, draining the color and the anger from Pat's face. His eyes were wells of pain.

"My gift isn't a big deal," he said. "It isn't big enough to matter."

"Will you stop twisting everything I say?" she cried, choking back tears. She wanted to strike out at him for all his obstinacy, but contented herself with shouting, "I meant that nothing should be strong enough to come between us."

Pat stared at her silently.

Clutching, agonizing fear forced out more words. "I love everything you've given me, Pat. Everything. Your smile. Your touch. Your jokes. You."

"Everything?" he asked, still staring. "How about the pain, Camilla?"

"What pain?"

"Don't pretend. I know I've hurt you, I've failed you."

She hadn't the faintest idea what he was talking about; all she knew was that her fear was growing, consuming everything until she could scarcely breathe, scarcely see.

He stared at her for a long moment, his eyes filled with something she couldn't name. Pain? Fear?

Regret? Then he turned aside and slowly began putting his things back into the suitcase.

"Is it that important for you to unpack your own things?" she asked, trying with humor to ease the terror clawing at her.

He spoke without looking up at her. "You have a dark, oppressive cloud in your life. I am going to remove it. That's the least I can do for you."

"What are you talking about?"

"Don't ever accept pain," he continued. "You don't deserve it."

"Would you stop playing Keats and Shelley and talk like a regular person?"

"They're English," Pat said. "I'm Irish."

Dusty's anger boiled over. She hurt too much to try to control it. "Damm it," she screamed. "Stop playing games with me and talk straight."

"I'm leaving," he said, still not looking up at her. He went into the bathroom and came back with his toilet articles. He put them into the bag and closed it. "It's the only thing I have left to give you. I can't think of anything else that would bring sunshine into your life."

He couldn't think of anything else! Where had he been for the last few weeks? "Let me give you a hint, you big oaf." Her voice was harsh and loud, and tears were streaming down her face, but she didn't care anymore. "I want you. No money, no jewels, no furs. Just you and your big strong arms around me."

He picked up the suitcase and stood there a moment. "You deserve better."

"There is no one better," she cried.

He slowly walked to the door, and desperation raced through her, lending her energy and strength to fight back, a rage to break down his stubbornness.

She ran after him, pounding him on the shoulders and back with her fists, trying to get him to turn around, to look at her, really look at her.

"I said there's no one better than you. Damn you, Pat Mahoney. You have no right to decide who's good for me and who's not." He just kept on walking. "You hear me? You have no right."

They reached the front door and Dusty had no more strength, no more fight. The fiery rage had burned itself out as suddenly as it had come. She couldn't cry or hit or do anything but lean against the wall. She reached out her hand to touch his arm. "Pat?" All her love, her need, her fear and desperation were in that one word.

Still, he didn't look at her. His gaze was on the door. "Good-bye, Camilla," he said quietly.

She stared, unable to believe this was really happening, that his hand was really reaching for the doorknob. "Aren't you going to kiss me? Or just hold me a little?"

"I've hurt you enough already." He pulled open the door and was gone.

Dusty sank to the floor, silent tears washing her face.

She felt empty and tired. All feeling had been wrung out of her, the very life drained from her body. For the last hour or so she had alternated between rage and tears. Now she was a zombie, with nothing left to give.

In a few short weeks Pat had become her life, and now he was gone. How was she supposed to live without him? She'd exist. She'd breathe and eat and go to work, but the smile would be gone. Laughter and beauty and sunshine were all meaningless now.

The sound of the buzzer caused her to jump up from the kitchen table, where she'd been staring into a cup of tea. Hope struggled in the desert of her soul as she raced to the door.

"Yes?"

A familiar voice came up through the static. "Camilla? It's Dad."

What was wrong? She quickly buzzed him in and opened her door. "Dad?" she called down from the top of the stairs. "What's wrong? What are you doing here?"

He stopped halfway up, looking at her. "I don't know. You tell me what's wrong."

"Dad." She eased a long, slow sigh past her lips. "I've had a long weekend and I'm really not up to playing games. Please tell me why you decided to come visit me at"—she looked quickly at her watch— "twenty minutes past midnight on a Sunday night. No, I guess it's really Monday morning."

"Pat told me to."

"He what?" Energy flowed into her body and gave her voice strength.

"Yeah," her father said. "He called and said that you were all alone and that I should come over and take care of you."

"Take care of me?" She had thought that she was empty, but a hidden residue of anger exploded. "I'm an adult, a competent woman, and I don't need anybody to take care of me. You men can all go to hell."

She stomped back into her apartment, her anger swirling through her like a flame.

"Are you throwing me out?"

She turned to see the concerned expression on her

father's face. A suitcase, with a shirttail hanging out, was in his hand. The collar of a pajama top peeked over the rumpled collar of his shirt.

The anger burned out quickly as love soothed her frayed nerves. Her father had risen from a sound sleep and hurried here to be with her. How could she be angry at him? She buried her face in his shoulder and let him hug her until she could hardly breathe.

Slowly he released her and studied her face with a frown. "You okay?"

She nodded and waited in silence for the lump in her throat to dissolve. When she could talk she asked, "Want some tea?"

He shook his head as he came in and closed the door. "My old nerves don't handle caffeine too well. Especially this time of the night."

"It's herbal tea," she hastened to assure him. "Caffeine-free."

"Okay, I'll give it a try then."

"What kind do you want?" She'd almost said that Pat had stocked a wide range, but she couldn't say his name. Not yet. "I have all kinds. Cinnamon apple, strawberry royal, lemon."

There was a doubtful look on her father's face. "I'll have some lemon. That sounds safest."

He followed Dusty into the kitchen and sat in silence while she made the tea. It wasn't until they were sitting before steaming cups that she spoke.

"Pat's left me," she said.

Her father didn't look surprised. "Yeah. He said he had to."

"He did not," she protested, her anger flaring up again. "That sounds like I threw him out. He left because he wanted to."

"Sometimes it ain't what a man wants to do; it's what he has to do."

She tried to stamp out her irritation by sipping slowly at her tea, but it didn't work. The scalding liquid only made her hurt more, and she put up thicker walls of anger to block out the pain.

"Pat and I were more than employer and employee."

Her father just nodded.

"I thought we had been very discreet."

"It's like trying to hide spring." A smile softened his features.

Dusty looked down into her cup. What an apt way to put it. Pat did bring spring to her. She'd felt a rebirth, a sense of coming alive and blossoming. But the fates were denying her summer and fall and throwing her straight into the harsh, bitter cold of midwinter.

"He's so moody," she told her tea. "They talk about women having mood swings. Well, I don't think all the women in the world could cover the range that Pat Mahoney could handle in five minutes."

"It wasn't an easy situation for him, honey."

"I tried to be understanding."

"I doubt that it was anything you did. When you're a young man, you want to give your sweetheart the sun, the moon, and the stars. You find out soon enough that you can't, and learn to settle for more mundane things like food and paying the electric bills. When you aren't even doing that—" He shrugged. "Well, I guess Pat just couldn't live with the guilt, the sense of failing you."

"A woman ought to be able to give too." Vacations. Dinner at nice restaurants. That new camel's-hair sport coat sitting in her closet that was meant to replace Pat's worn tweed on his birthday next week.

"A woman has to give just her love. That's all a man wants."

Dusty had to work at keeping calm. Her anger was ready to explode again. "That's all a woman wants from a man. That's all I needed from Pat."

"True, but he needed to give you more."

"Yeah, I know," she said bitterly. "The sun, the moon, and the stars."

"That's the way it's always been, baby."

"Baloney." Dusty snorted. "That's not the way it ought to be."

"I know, I know." Her father got stiffly to his feet and took their empty cups to the sink. "Why don't we hit the sack? The morning sunshine always puts a better glow on things, and you look like you need a few z's."

Reluctantly she pushed herself up from the table. His arms engulfed her in a quick bear hug, then he steered her down the hall to her room.

"You got any early appointments?" he asked.

She shook her head. "The first thing I have is a luncheon date."

"Then set your alarm for ten," he ordered.

Damn. Was that what men needed women for? Someone to order around? But she was too tired to argue, and just nodded as she dragged herself into her bedroom. Actually, getting up at ten wasn't a bad idea.

Eleven

"Hello, Camilla," an old lady called, looking up from where she was scrubbing her front steps.

"Morning, Mrs. Rosonova," Dusty called back.

A young Oriental woman with a solemn, almond-eyed little girl in a stroller smiled at Dusty and her father as they passed on the sidewalk.

"You're getting chummy with your neighbors all of a sudden," Dusty's father said under his breath. "What happened? You giving up the corporate rat race to join the human race?"

"Very funny." She climbed into the passenger side of his car and waited until he was settled in at the driver's seat. "I've never been unfriendly."

"No, that would require time. You've just always been too busy to notice the rest of the world." He pulled away from the curb and they rode in silence for a long moment. "Until recently."

Dusty stared out her window, knowing her father

was attributing her change in attitude to Pat's departure a few weeks ago, but that was nonsense. True, Pat had pointed out the wonderful variety of the neighborhood and the reasons to cherish its diversity, but that had nothing to do with her now. May was always a beautiful month, and she was just getting out more, planting some flowers along the front sidewalk, taking walks, shopping in the local stores. It was only to be expected that she'd meet more of her neighbors.

She clutched at the briefcase lying in her lap and got her mind back in gear. "Are all your partners going to be at my presentation?" she asked her father.

"Yeah," he said, keeping his eyes on the road. "The whole lot of them." He slowed for a red light and paused. "I'm just a minority partner myself, and so is Lisa, who's lining up the merchants. Our architect and our restaurant man both put up one hundred thousand each. They've got a lot staked on the success of this shopping center."

"I can't see any reason why it won't do well, especially if I can secure that location for them."

She had been surprised when her father had come to her the week before and told her about this partnership he was in, and their decision to hire a commercial real estate agent. Her enthusiasm for new projects had been at an all-time low, but she'd agreed to make a presentation to his group. Her father had been so excited about steering work her way that she hadn't had the heart to refuse.

"We're operating out of the architect's basement right now," her father said.

"Gotta start someplace," Dusty remarked. If she forced herself to sound cheerful, maybe it would become a habit in twenty or thirty years.

The modern town-house complex where they stopped blended in well with the old brownstones on the street. They walked through the complex, into a town house near the back and down a half-flight of stairs into what was planned to be a basement recreation room. Now it served as an office for busy people who needed twice the space.

"Hi, folks," her father called out. "This here's my little girl. She's all set to tell us how she'll give us a hand."

Dusty resisted the temptation to bop him on the head for his little-girl remark and smiled at the people who came to greet her. Ken Barton, the bespectacled architect, introduced his redheaded wife Jan, who was the group's office manager, and a tall, older woman, Lisa, who was signing up the retail stores for the shopping center.

"Where's Pat? He ought to be here," Lisa said, and glanced around her before turning back to Dusty. "He's the one finding restaurants for the center."

Pat? Her Pat? But this one was a majority partner with a hundred grand invested, not an ambitionless drifter. A crowd of jumbled emotions grabbed her stomach and twisted it. She smiled vacantly at the graying lawyer whose name she had totally missed, and looked for her father. He was busily setting up chairs for her presentation, and too engrossed in the finer points of his task to look her way. It had to be her Pat.

She took a deep breath and let it ease some of her angry confusion. Did it matter to her that Pat was really a businessman, not a butler? No, she could even understand why he had taken the job with her— flexible hours, room and board, good location. What she couldn't see, and what hurt so much, was why he hadn't told her the truth. No, that was wrong. She did know why, there was only one possible reason: He didn't care about her as she had cared about him.

She began to set up her portable presentation stand as she chatted with the others. She was a professional and could put aside her own hurts in order to do a good job. Pat's presence would not affect her at all. The small room echoed with laughter and conversation, and she seemed to be the only one conscious of the sudden footsteps coming down the stairs. Loud as thunder, they seemed to overpower all else, yet the laughter and talk went on. Her hands tensed and she paged through her notes a third time.

Love. Anger. Fear. Desire. All tugging and pulling at her like wolves at a deer carcass. Why had she agreed to do this? Why hadn't she suspected that there was something behind that smile of her father's? She wasn't prepared to see Pat again. It had been too long. No, not long enough. Hell, she couldn't even think straight. Damn her father's meddling.

"Hello, Camilla."

Her cool, professional business manner teetered on the edge of a precipice. Dusty grabbed it, desperately pulling it back into place. Through sheer will power she kept the businessperson in place.

"Hello, Pat." The words were strained, but she could speak. The woman in her wanted to cry out, but she was given no opportunity.

"You're looking fine, Camilla."

She paused. His eyes had a touch of shadow under them, but otherwise they seemed fine too. Not lively, but certainly not filled with tragedy. The brown hair was still unruly, and that magnificent body wasn't missing his exercise equipment, which was still stored at the apartment. Or her, a tiny voice pointed out.

"I was going to introduce you two." The architect chuckled. "But that doesn't appear to be necessary."

"Oh, no," Dusty's father assured him heartily. "They used to live together."

Great timing, Dad. She tried to smile at the four pairs of eyes that turned to her.

She cleared her throat. "Mr. Mahoney used to work for me."

More silence.

"He served as a butler/houseman," she clarified.

"Oh."

"Yeah, Pat told us about that."

Did he? "Well," Dusty said, jumping in briskly now that there was no more to be said about that, "let's talk about what you want to hear. Real estate and the services my company can provide you."

Dusty ignored her dry mouth and sweaty hands, plowing ahead with her presentation. She told them a little of her background and her company's, then went on to what she could do for them. Her eyes kept wanting to stray to Pat, to watch for that gleam in his eye, to tease a smile from his reluctant lips, but she was strong. Her mind was in control, not her eyes.

She had survived seeing him again, survived learning that he'd kept a major part of his life hidden from her, and she would continue to survive and get stronger. Now that she had passed the initial exam, though, there was no reason to keep retesting herself. She didn't need his presence to convince herself of victory. She was over him, she told herself firmly.

"Those present owners ain't budging on their asking price," her father pointed out.

"Yes, I checked into that."

"They're giving us a lot of stuff about what good shape the building is in," the architect added.

"Which is ridiculous," Dusty said. "If there were a number of firms who needed a bicycle plant, they'd have a case. As it is, yours is the only serious offer they have. Price is based on demand, and they haven't got any."

"But what if they won't come down?" Jan asked.

"They will. First we'll look into getting the zoning changed. That won't be any problem with those soccer fields you're putting in." They were setting aside a large corner of the land for a neighborhood park that would have soccer fields as well as a number of other facilities. "The city'll love the community recreational area you're making. It's a lot better than the eyesore that the property's become. Once the zoning's changed, the tax structure will change too. They'll sell."

"But how long will it take?" Lisa asked. "I'm having trouble keeping all my merchants hanging around, and I'm sure Pat's having the same trouble with the restaurants."

They all looked at Pat, who grunted something she supposed was an affirmative.

"I think this project will really be rolling in a month," Dusty assured them. "You've got a great idea and a unique one. All I need to get things going is a signature on this exclusive agreement and we'll be on our way." Dusty took a contract out of her briefcase.

They each glanced briefly at the paper, and passed it on, ending with the lawyer. He nodded. "It's the standard contract. You don't pay anything unless they produce. I don't see any problem with it."

It was signed and they shook hands all around. Or

almost all around. She noted that Pat hung back. Not that it bothered her. He was a majority partner and could have vetoed the contract if he'd chosen. The fact that he hadn't was approval enough for her. She didn't need to shake his hand for added reassurance. She packed up her briefcase, folded up her presentation stand, and looked around for her father.

"Be with you in a minute, honey," he called from his huddle at a far table with the architect.

She nodded.

"How have you been?"

Her heart stopped, but by the time she turned to face Pat a smile was on her face. "Fine," she said. "And you?"

He only shrugged. "Is your father still staying with you?"

"For a few more days. He's eager to get back to his house. You know, he doesn't like to leave it empty."

Pat's frown deepened. "I don't like the idea of your being there along."

She was tempted to invite him back. Or point out that he was the one who'd left. Or tell him to go to hell. She did none of them, however, just glared in her father's direction, wishing he'd hurry up.

"The group seemed pleased with all you'll be able to do for us."

Wasn't he pleased also? "Yes, I'm working for you now. You ought to find that turn of events amusing."

"Camilla."

"Hey, it'll be great. You can order me around, make me do things your way, and fire me when you get tired of having me about. You ought to be thrilled. Most people don't get their chance at revenge so neatly handed to them."

He raked his hand through his hair, and the action

tugged at her heart. She remembered the feel of that thick hair between her fingers as she sought the warmth of his lips, remembered how it had felt to have those hands running through her hair, brushing it back from her neck so that his mouth could— She threw those thoughts out bodily and slammed the door of her mind to keep them out.

"I never wanted revenge," he told her. "I liked working for you."

"Oh?"

"You were easy to work for," he explained, correcting himself at her mocking glance. "Not nearly as demanding as you could have been."

His voice trailed away as her face burned. She remembered, even if he didn't, their trip to Galena. How he had teased her about demanding his sexual services.

"Why didn't you tell me about this partnership of yours?" she asked suddenly. She hadn't meant to ask him, but she needed to know.

"What difference would it have made? It wouldn't have changed anything."

Sure, it would have. She wouldn't have this gnawing pain now, mocking her former belief that they had been close. She'd still be alone though; that much wouldn't have changed. "You were the one who was always so concerned about titles," she pointed out. "I would have thought you'd have preferred businessman to butler."

"It wouldn't have mattered which title I gave myself. I still was failing you."

Her father was finally approaching, and Dusty could have hugged him in relief if she weren't already so irritated with his trickery. "Yeah, I know," she said bitterly, casting a quick look up at Pat. "The sun, the moon, and the stars."

Pat stared blankly at her. She picked up her things and passed by him to get to the stairs. "Nice meeting you all," she called out to the group in general, though her gaze stayed far from Pat. "I'll be in touch." With them, not him. Their touching days were over.

"Dinnertime."

Pat looked up from the financial statements he was studying. He hadn't realized it was that late already. The day was almost over and he'd hardly accomplished anything. That meeting with Camilla this morning had thrown him off schedule.

"I'm really sorry, Jan," he said, getting to his feet. "Fine guest I am. Foist myself on you two in the middle of the night weeks ago and now I can't even offer to help with meals."

Jan just laughed and patted his cheek. "I didn't want your help today," she assured him. "I felt like planning my own celebration feast."

"Celebration? What are we celebrating?"

"Are you kidding?" Ken followed him up the stairs to the kitchen. "The fact that our ships have come in. That soon we'll be rolling in money."

Pat frowned at their misguided excitement. "If you mean our hiring of Miss Ross, don't you think you're being a bit premature? She hasn't done anything yet."

"But she will." Ken sounded positive. "She will."

Pat mumbled something that even he couldn't understand, and followed Ken to the table. Lisa and their lawyer, Frank, were already seated; Jan must have invited everyone to stay for the celebration dinner.

Unfortunately not all present were in the mood for celebrating. Seeing Camilla again had stirred up feelings in Pat that were best ignored. His desires for Camilla were churning around inside him, his needs growing and consuming him until she was all he thought about, all he saw. He took his place at the modern Scandinavian-style dining table.

"Is this one of Pat's recipes?" Frank asked as Jan brought a casserole to the table.

"Nope," Jan answered. "It's one hundred percent Jan Barton."

Pat forced a smile to his face in acknowledgment. Then, keeping the smile there, he left his companions and sank into his own dark world. How would he be able to work with Camilla every day? It had been hard enough before he knew he loved her. Where would he get the strength to turn aside from her beauty? Where would he get the courage to deny the pounding of his heart?

"Don't you like it? Jan asked.

Pat tried to lift himself up out of his personal abyss. "Oh, the food's delicious," he assured her. "Absolutely delicious. I just don't seem to have much appetite tonight." He picked up his wineglass and sipped at the burgundy.

"You know, I had the impression that your Camilla was an older woman," Lisa said to him.

All eyes were on him, and he returned the wineglass to the table. The Mahoney clan did not breed cowards. "I don't believe I ever mentioned her age." Or claimed ownership.

"No, you didn't," Lisa agreed. "But people form

impressions based on what's said, and I pictured an older woman, cold and maybe a little ruthless."

His Camilla cold and ruthless? "You should listen to what people are really saying instead of letting your imagination draw wild pictures," he snapped.

Their silent stares stopped any other comments he might have made.

"I have to agree with Lisa," Jan said. "I had pictured a completely different Camilla from the one who spoke to us today."

"I'm sorry my descriptive powers are so shabby," he muttered. The rolls were passed around the table, then the butter.

"Tell me, how does one get a job as butler for such a doll?" Frank asked.

"Miss Ross is not a doll," Pat said. "She is a lady, a fine lady."

"Perfect for the full-service butler," Ken said.

In the blink of an eye black storm clouds surrounded him, thunder crashed in his ears, and waves pounded the shore. He leaped to his feet. "And what is that supposed to mean?"

Blank, startled faces stared back at him.

"Easy, Pat," Ken said quietly. "I didn't mean anything. You're the one who calls yourself a full-service butler."

The clouds parted to let light though not sunshine through. Lord, would he ever be free of her spell? Would her image ever stop calling to him?

"I'm sorry," Pat said. "My emotions just hit a downdraft, but I'll be fine." Their eyes held something too close to pity to suit his wishes and he stepped back from the table. "If you folks will excuse me, I think I'll go out for a breath of air."

Jan followed him to the door. "Are you sure you're all right, Pat?" she asked.

"I'm fine," he assured her. "We Irish know you can't enjoy the view from the mountain until you've experienced the lows of the valley." Before she had a chance to argue he had let himself out into the evening.

His brisk steps soon worked up a light sweat and had him feeling better. Or at least not so murderous, though there was no denying that he was drained. The poets had all warned him love was a treacherous sea to navigate. The trouble was he was caught in a whirlpool in the middle, and he'd never be reaching that beautiful paradise on the other side.

Spring had started so beautifully. Meeting Camilla. Getting to know her. To love her. She had become a part of him, and now that she was gone, it was as if the seas were washing over him, pulling him down to their murky depths. His love for Camilla decreed that they be together forever. His circumstances denied it.

The flame of irritation raised his temperature a few degrees. Soon she would be finding someone new. He hoped she did, he assured himself over the painful twisting of his gut. They had no future, and someone as lovely as Camilla shouldn't be alone. She deserved a fine man, a family around her, and a life of happiness.

He saw her before him, a swirling vision with a babe in her arms and love in her eyes for a hazy figure at her side. A figure that would never be himself. The rage, the despair, the fear in him, fought to be let free.

The closest thing to his anger was a red, white, and blue tricycle with a huge front wheel. His kick sent it rolling a few feet to the right of the sidewalk, another kick tipped it on its side. His anger was not abated, just mixed with shame. It was like kicking a bairn. He didn't feel more of a man for all his rage. He righted the little bike and went on.

He had to face facts. He couldn't marry Camilla, as much as his body ached for her, as much as his heart cried out that they belonged to each other. He was living off savings right now, and rapidly dwindling ones at that. There was no way he could offer her the life she deserved. And by the time he was ready to give her a home, she would be long-since married.

"Hey, Paddy."

Pat stopped and waited for the three boys who were running to catch up with him. He had walked the few miles between Ken's house and Camilla's neighborhood without even noticing.

"Good evening, gentlemen," he said.

"Hey, we been hearing about a shopping center going into the old bike plants. Heard you're one of the bigshots."

"I'm working with some people on it," Pat admitted.

"Gonna be a lot of jobs, eh, Paddy?"

"It'll be a while yet before everything is in place," Pat told them. "Probably enough time for all of you to finish high school."

They laughed nervously.

"I mean it," he said. "You come around without those diplomas and I'll have you bums thrown out."

"We're cool, Paddy."

"Yeah. I only got one year to go. I can do that time with my eyes closed."

"Get something out of it," Pat growled as he moved down the street. "Don't just put in your time."

Companionable laughter and hearty farewells followed him. His relationship with the neighborhood boys was improving by leaps and bounds. They were like boys the world over, desperately needing an outlet for all their surplus energy.

Had that been what Camilla was to him, an outlet for his surplus energy? No, she was much more than that. She was everything that was wonderful in the world. All the sweetness and gentleness. She was life and love and wonder, but she needed to be protected from the pain of the world. He'd give half his life for the right to be able to do that, but it was impossible. The laughing gods had taken the sails from his ship, leaving him to the mercy of the tossing waves.

Pat stopped at the next corner to lean against the streetlight. It had gotten dark while he was walking, but the circle of light shed no answers on his problems. If only he had money, the world would be his.

He straightened up suddenly. Where was his mind these days? He couldn't marry Camilla without money, so he'd get money. He'd get back the $100,000 that he had invested in the shopping center. It'd make things tight for the others, but not impossible. Camilla's father's arrival had eased things, and he himself had arranged excellent financing for the project. He and Camilla would reach that paradise of love after all.

Twelve

"I'll get it, Dad." Dusty grabbed the phone. "Hello. May I help you, please?"

"Good evening, Miss Ross. This is Pat. May I speak to your father, please."

Her heart faltered at the lilting sound of Pat's voice, but luckily her tongue didn't. "Certainly," she replied, her tone cool and crisp. "Just a moment."

She handed the phone to her father and busied herself with making powdered lemonade. Two scoops to a quart. Sounded easy enough, even with the distraction of her father's affirmative grunting. She measured the powder with precision and stuck the pitcher under the faucet. She didn't care if Pat called her father. He could call him every night if he wanted to. Twice a night even. She was getting on with her life.

Water rushed over the sides of the pitcher, washing lemonade powder into the sink with it. She turned off the faucet with an angry glare at her father's back. Did he have to take his calls in the kitchen and distract her?

By the time the next pitcher was made, her father was off the phone and ready for his glass. "That was Pat."

Dusty gave her own noncommittal grunt.

"He was asking my permission to come over and talk to you."

"He asked your permission to talk to me?" She took a deep breath.

"I told him it was okay."

"Okay?" She paced around the kitchen. "That man is insane. He comes from another planet. He's an alien."

"Ireland is a country, Camilla. Ain't they teaching you anything in college?"

She closed her eyes tight, clenched her fists, and leaned her head against the kitchen cabinets. She didn't want to talk to Pat. She didn't want to see him. He was bound up in his own little world and there was no place for the two of them in it.

"What does he want?" she asked. How long would she have to pretend that the sight of him didn't cause her pain?

"I don't know." Her father shrugged. "He wants to talk to you."

"Then why did he talk to you first?"

Her father might have been deaf for all the attention he paid to her question. "You know," he mused, "you don't have guys doing that anymore, asking the father's permission, I mean. Most guys don't consider a girl's father important anymore. Pat's old-fashioned, but I guess that's what makes him so nice."

Was this a paid political announcement or just another of her father's tricks? "I am going to scream," she said in a slow, deliberate voice.

The buzzer sounded, and her father got up. "Why don't you go put some shoes on instead? I'll get the door."

She didn't bother to argue the little points, saving her anger and frustration for what was coming. "This is a dream," she muttered as she stomped into the bedroom. "A horrible dream. A nightmare."

She opened her closet. The pumps wouldn't go with her shorts. Should she change into something more formal? She hadn't invited Pat, so why should she change? Besides, he'd be wearing his usual slacks and sport shirt. Anything more and those beautiful muscles would be hidden. She slipped into some loafers. Then she kicked them off. The hell with it. She was going to be comfortable.

"Camilla," her father called. "You have a guest."

"I'm coming," she snapped. She slipped into a pair of sandals. At least her feet would be comfortable, even if she wasn't. Stopping at the mirror, she took a deep breath, put on her stern business face, and walked regally into the living room.

"Good evening, Camilla," Pat said.

Oh, damn! Double-damn even. Pat was wearing a dark suit, tie, and white shirt, and his hair appeared to have been terrorized into submission. He could use his shiny wing tips for mirrors and his usual five o'clock shadow was nowhere to be seen. In his hand were several long-stemmed roses. Dusty's bare toes tried desperately to hide behind the thin straps of her sandals.

"Say hello to your guest, Camilla," her father prompted. "Maybe he'd like something to drink."

"I can handle it, Dad."

"You should put the flowers in a vase with some water."

"I said I can handle it, Dad."

She took the flowers from Pat. "Can I get you anything to drink?"

"Something to cool the palates would be wonderful." His smile almost took her breath away, but she was prepared for such trickery and had stopped breathing the moment she'd seen him.

"Why don't I get us some lemonade?" she suggested. "I'll put these in a vase." She shot a quick glare at her father and added, "With some water."

The air in the kitchen was more conducive to breathing, so she paused a minute to let some oxygen into her lungs. Her heart was racing along at a ridiculous rate. If this was going to be her reaction to Pat every time she saw him, she was going to die of a heart attack soon. Or asphyxiation. She might love him, but that didn't mean that her body had to fall apart whenever he was near.

She took a deep breath, evicted the sentimentality from her being, and went over to the cabinets to get a vase. Her hand stopped, suspended in midair. Where were the vases now? Did she even have any? She was about to call for Pat, but she caught herself in time. He didn't work for her anymore.

Starting at one end, she began looking through the cabinets. Pat was too much a gentleman to buy her cut flowers if he knew that she didn't have a vase. Or was he? As she drew closer to the end of the row of cabinets, the vehemence with which she closed the doors grew. That bastard was probably smirking away in her living room. It would take the twisted mind of a Pat Mahoney to buy her cut flowers when he knew damn good and well that she didn't have a vase.

She found the vases in the last cabinet and shook her head at the fiendish genius of the man. The roses were placed vigorously in the container, and water added.

Now for the lemonade. The sooner she brought it to him, the sooner he'd be going. And the sooner she could have a good cry. She turned quickly to get glasses, but her sandal caught in some strange way on the foot of the kitchen table. Holding herself upright, with one hand on the table, Dusty held her foot with the other and bit her lip to keep from screaming. When the pain subsided she angrily threw the sandals across the room.

It took her a while to find some nice glasses, but nowhere near as long as it had taken to find the vase. She put ice and lemonade in each glass and then stared at the three glasses. There was a tray around someplace, but she didn't know whether Pat had it in the kitchen or in the dining room cabinet. She was not, however, looking for another stupid item. Wrapping her fingers around the three glasses, she clutched them to her chest and walked rapidly into the living room.

"Grab one before they all drop," she ordered her father.

He blinked in surprise, but took a glass quickly enough.

Then, putting a broad smile on her face, she turned to Pat. "Mr. Mahoney," she said sweetly, and gave him a glass. She sat down, crossed her right leg over her left, waved her bare foot nonchalantly in the air, and smiled brightly at the two men.

After a lengthy pause her father broke the silence. "Pat and I had a nice talk, honey."

That was wonderful. She was glad Pat had nice talks with somebody, although talking hadn't been her favorite activity with him. There was laughing, hugging, kissing, loving—

She grabbed her lemonade and gulped at it, her eyes shooting fire at her father. If this was another of his tricks, another of his little "accidents," she was going to disown him.

Her father stood up quickly as if reading the threats in her glare. "Pat said he wanted to talk to you. I got some work to do." From the doorway he called back. "I'll take my drink with me. Glad you had a chance to drop by, Pat."

Silence came again and took her father's empty seat.

"How have you been, Camilla?"

"Fine. And you?"

"Fine. Just fine."

There was silence again.

"To tell the honest-to-God truth, Camilla, I'm not fine at all."

"Oh?"

"I rattle around the corners of loneliness looking for my soul." His voice was quiet. "It finally penetrated my thick skull that it would never be mine again. I'd left it here with you."

Dusty watched him, her eyes trying to read his, trying to see what it was he was actually saying. Was he asking to come back? Her breath seemed to have stopped as hope came alive within her. Pat moved to sit down next to her on the sofa, the fabric of his pants rough against her skin. Breathing was out of the question; she had forgotten how.

"I had to leave, Camilla."

His hand took possession of hers. The warmth of his touch eased life back into her frozen limbs.

"I was never sure you understood," he said. "It wasn't that I didn't care for you; it was that I cared so much."

Were her ears really hearing this or was this some fantastic dream created from her desperate need and loneliness? "My father explained it," she told Pat. "He said that a man wants to give a woman the sun, the moon, and the stars, but settles for paying the rent."

"I couldn't even do that," Pat said. His eyes were dark and troubled, hungry for her understanding. "And it was eating me up. I needed you, but I needed to be a man too."

The strength of his grip on her hand, clutching as if he'd never let go, freed the words from her tongue. "So why are you back now?"

He left her side, his sheltering presence gone, but he didn't go far enough to let her fears and loneliness return. He just slipped to one knee before her. His eyes looked deep into hers. The light she saw flickering deep within him seemed to promise to slay her loneliness forever. His hand still held hers tightly.

"I'm here to tell you that I love you more than life itself, and nothing would make me happier in this whole world than if you'd agree to be my wife."

Sudden ecstatic joy washed over her like sunshine showering a flower with warmth. "Pat!"

"No, don't say anything yet," he said quickly, before she threw her arms about him. "Just let me explain. Hear me out first."

What was there to explain beyond the fact that he loved her and wanted to marry her? Her heart wanted to cry out in joy, her lips wanted to laugh and sing,

she wanted to wrap her body around Pat's and celebrate their love. She did none of that, though, just
raised her hand gently to his face and touched his
cheek, trying to convince herself this really was
happening.

"I've got it all figured out," he said. "And you don't
have to worry. You're probably thinking that ladies
don't marry their butlers or that I'm not much of a
businessman yet, but I'll be able to take care of you as
I ought."

A cloud threw its shadow across her face and her
joy. "Take care of me? How?"

"Like a man takes care of his wife. He buys a home,
pays the bills, supports her and their children." His
voice quickened; he seemed determined to make her
understand. "I saw my own mother work herself to
death in the factories and with odd jobs trying to help
my father meet the bills. I swore I'd never let that happen to my wife."

There was a stubborn set to his jaw, and as much
as Dusty longed to throw herself into his arms and
lose herself in his embrace, she held back.

"Pat, what's changed? You left here a few weeks ago
without the means to support a family. What have
you done since then? Robbed a bank? Your money's
all tied up in the shopping center project."

"Not for much longer."

She saw where he was heading. "You can't take it
out," she cried. The shadowy cloud of fear came
closer. "That project's a part of you and your appreci-
ation of this area's past. How can you even think of
stopping it?"

"It's not that important to me anymore," he argued.
"Not as important as you are. But the project won't
suffer. I'm not taking out the money all at once. I'll be

giving up my partnership now, but the group will return the funds gradually. I'll get a job as a chef, and between that and my savings, I'll take good care of you."

By letting her bear the burden of his abandoned hopes and dreams? "I'm not helpless," she pointed out. "I can take care of myself. All I want is your love."

His eyes were fierce with stubbornness, and she didn't know how to reach him. She slid her arms around his neck, bringing them close together. There was a fire deep in his eyes, beyond all the pride, that reflected her own hunger. Her lips teased his, then clung to them for a long moment of need. "All I want is your love," she whispered as she pulled back slightly. "Just love me, Pat. Just love me."

His inner fire flared up, his eyes alive with its burning, and she thought it would consume them both. His hands reached out to her, pulling her against him, tighter and closer. He wanted her. He needed her. She thought she had won, but then the obstinacy took hold of his jaw and spread throughout his entire person. He pulled away from her and stood up.

"We've been through this all before. A man takes care of those he loves."

She flew to her feet. "Buffalo chips!"

Anger replaced stubbornness on his face. Reason was what was needed, not anger. She took a deep breath, thought of the wonderful moments they'd spent in the radiance of their love, and forced peace into her voice.

"Pat, please," she begged. "Don't put me on a pedestal. I get nosebleeds when I'm up too high."

Her attempt at humor touched him, and a sliver of confusion came into his eyes.

"I've never doubted you as a man," she said softly.

"And the more I learn about you, the more exciting I find you. You're taking big risks and trying to build a business and contribute to your community all at the same time. You're an entrepreneur, Pat. American women find that very exciting."

His lips still had that determined twist, and his eyes were watchful. She mustered her troops for one last charge.

"That business is your dream, Pat. What kind of woman would I be if I let you throw that away?"

"It's my decision," he insisted.

"No, it isn't." Her voice was rising again, and she had to fight to keep it steady. "A marriage is a partnership, and this potential partner votes no to the proposal that Patrick Mahoney destroy his dreams."

He kept his gaze away from her by turning to stare out the window. She couldn't tell from the tension in his wide shoulders if he was giving in to her or giving up on her. If only he'd let their love speak for itself. If she just had one night to convince him!

"A man takes care of his wife," he repeated obstinately.

"Then don't marry me," she cried. "We can live together until your money starts coming in, then you can marry me."

"A man marries the woman he loves."

She sighed and sank down onto the sofa again. "Pat, we're getting nowhere." Why couldn't he listen to reason?

He turned to face her. "No, you're right, we aren't. I guess the sun wasn't smiling on our love after all."

Before she had time to cry out, or stop him, he left, his footsteps echoing down the stairs even as she rushed after him. By the time she had her apartment door pulled open, the door downstairs was being shut. He was gone.

"Pat!" she cried out, more in desperation than in expectation that he'd hear. She slammed the door. The big, stubborn oaf. She should have known he'd go poetic on her.

She stomped across the room and threw herself into a chair. She could understand his pride and appreciate his old-fashioned ways. But couldn't he bend a little now? He could support her all he wanted later if it was so important to him, but couldn't he take a little from her now?

At least he had admitted he loved her. That was a step in the right direction. All she had to do was get him to change his mind about the rest. How hard could that be for someone who'd fought to get what she wanted for the last twenty-nine years?

Camilla led the boys into Jan and Ken's town house and guided them down the stairs to the makeshift office. "Just put the boxes down anywhere here," she told them, and pressed some dollar bills into their hands. "Thanks a lot, guys," she called after them. Her heart was flying high as a kite, and her voice sounded as if it were in the clouds also.

"Camilla?"

Dusty spun around to smile into her father's confused face. And no wonder he was confused. She had arrived early for her meeting, and with her were some large plastic bags and several boxes.

"Hi, Dad." She kissed his cheek, put her briefcase down on a nearby table, and smoothed the skirt of her cream-colored suit. It was a nervous gesture and not particularly satisfying since it didn't occupy her hands long enough. She brushed a speck of lint from her father's collar. "I know I'm early, but I hoped to talk to Pat for a few minutes."

"Oh, sure." Her father sounded as if this happened every day, but looked as if he feared she'd gone off the deep end without a life jacket. She flashed a quick smile at him, then looked around the room at the others. Jan and Ken were here, and so was Lisa. The lawyer wasn't. Pat, she knew without even seeing him, was over at the far desk. He got to his feet and walked uncertainly over to her.

Keeping a bright smile plastered to her face, Dusty ran a casual hand over her hair. Was it still in the soft curls she'd struggled to arrange? Did she have lipstick left in the middle of her lips, or had she wiped them clean with nervous licking?

Her whole life passed before her in the few seconds it took Pat to cover the length of the room. Her dedication to her work, to getting her degree. The hazy longings and vague dissatisfactions of the past. The feeling of completeness Pat had brought her. This was her last chance to get the sun, moon, and stars love promised. If she blew this, it was over.

"Hello, Camilla." Pat looked more wonderful than ever. She knew he couldn't have gotten taller or broader in the shoulder, since she'd seen him a few days ago, but he seemed bigger. His eyes seemed bluer, and his lips more tempting than she remembered.

She smiled at him, a Miss America smile designed to dazzle and delight, and, if nothing else, to give her some courage. "I thought as long as I was coming over here for a meeting, I'd bring some things you'd left behind."

"Left behind? You mean my weight set? You shouldn't have brought that, it's too heavy."

She laughed. Partly because he thought those teenage boys could carry his weight set, and partly because the atmosphere in the room needed a little levity. Her heart needed it. "No, it's not your weights."

She picked up the nearest bag, swallowed her heart, and pulled the twist-tie off. She'd never been a coward before, and this was not the time to start chickening out, not with Pat's love at stake. She dumped the contents of the bag out. Hundreds, thousands of suns filled the air, floating down to the floor and settling in smiling piles at Pat's feet. There were suns cut from yellow paper, from newspaper, from tissue paper. Cardboard ones, glittery ones, even a papier mâché one. Large ones, small ones. Fat ones, thin ones.

"What?" Pat was puzzled, and she smiled again. The suns' smiles put sunshine into her own heart. This would work. It had to.

The next bag held moons. A variety of kinds, mostly cut from paper, and no less in number than the suns. Half-moons, quarter-moons, full moons drifted through the silence to mingle with the suns on the floor. Harvest moons, lover's moons, and planting moons. A man in the moon grinned from his perch on the edge of a desk, and she grinned back.

"What is this?" Pat pushed the words out.

"Suns and moons," she said, and reached for a box. The ice in her hands had melted. What was there to fear in fighting for her love? Her father's chuckle dragged her gaze toward the back of the room. He gave her a thumb's-up signal, and she winked back, then ripped open the box, flinging its contents into the room.

Stars danced through the air. Small ones, less than an inch across, and huge foil-covered ones she'd bought in a store that specialized in department store decorations. Thick plastic ones that had wobbled atop spring antennae. Velvety ones that ironed onto shirts. Stars cut out of spongy material, star-shaped flowers. Even some star-shaped breakfast cereal.

The other bags and boxes held more of the same, and she opened them with glee, gaining enthusiasm from the stunned silence of the people staring at her. Only her father seemed to have any inkling of what was going on, and even he couldn't be sure.

Once everything was emptied, Dusty brushed off the stars clinging to her skirt. Several were stuck to Pat's jeans, but she didn't move to take them off. He was, after all, the star of the show. The stunned look on his face told her she had a few minutes to press her cause before he regained his voice. It was time to make use of her advantage.

"You seem to have this misguided notion that you've never given me anything," she began. Her voice was wobbly as she was a bit uncertain about pouring her heart out in front of all these people. She kept her eyes on Pat, where her heart was anyway. "You think that as things are there is nothing you can give me."

She kicked a foot, sending a spray of suns, moons, and stars into the air. "Somehow you missed the fact that you have given me all I ever wanted. In loving me you have already given me the sun, the moon, and the stars. There's no need for you to settle for mundane items like rent and food."

His eyes narrowed as he began to understand, so

she hurried ahead, afraid he was going to start the same old argument again.

"The trouble is, after you left, the shine went out of all this." She paused to wave a hand at the galaxy at his feet. "Without you there to keep the sun shining and the stars glowing, all this turned to paper and plastic."

She took a deep breath and dared a look around her. She had her audience behind her at any rate, though she had no clue as to Pat's feelings. "So, anyway, I'm giving all these back to you. No one can make them shine but you, and since you won't do that for me, I don't have any use for them."

She looked up at him, the hope in her eyes pleading with him. "I love you, but—"

"Camil—Dusty," he corrected himself. His voice was hoarse, choked by emotions or embarrassment, she didn't know which. She hadn't really thought of how he'd feel being on display like this.

It was too late for retreat. She plowed ahead with a grin and a shake of her head. "Camilla," she said. "Dusty's my dad."

He appeared not to notice her concession, and took her shoulders in his large hands as if he wanted to shake sense into her. He just held her, though, his fingers moving slightly, enjoying the contact with her. All couldn't be lost.

"Camilla, you just don't understand."

"Sure, I do. Finally I do. I finally figured the whole thing out." Her excitement spilled over into laughter, and she couldn't fight temptation anymore. She reached over and slid her arms around his waist, hugging him to her. He felt so good, so warm, so wonderful. "You're a bit old-fashioned, right?" She looked up at him, not about to let go. He'd have to pry her off.

He nodded.

"Well, I have the perfect old-fashioned solution for you. My job is my dowry."

"Your dowry?" Stubbornness was giving way to uncertainty in his voice.

"Sure, wives always used to bring a dowry to the marriage, so this'll be mine. Then, when you make your fortune in a few years, you can support me all you want." Her smile faltered just slightly at the frown in his eyes. "It's a wonderful solution, the perfect solution, the only solution," she said. "Unless you don't love me." Doubt swept over her, engulfing her and pulling her back from him.

His arms would not let her go. They tightened as hers loosened. "Unless I don't love you? And here I am dying for want of you." His eyes had that gleam, the warmth of love in them.

"Oh, Pat." Her voice was a breath, a sigh, the beginning of spring again.

His lips came down to meet hers and take her soaring into the stars. Past the sun and around the moon they flew, never stopping, never pausing until need for air finally drew them apart.

His kiss wasn't enough. She needed to hear him say the words. "Pat, I love you so much. Tell me everything's all right."

He pulled her back for another kiss, quicker, but no less potent. Her knees threatened to give out. Relief and desire swirled together to confuse her until all she could do was hold him tightly.

"I'm going to give you the best life possible, Camilla," he promised her, his eyes solemn. "I need you too much to let you go now, but I promise, when the money starts coming in I'm going to take care of you, as I want."

"Fine," she said. "Just don't make me wait around that long without you."

He laughed and held her away from him. "Why, Miss Ross, is that a proposition I'm hearing? What would my dear departed mother think?"

Camilla's cheeks ignited, not with the thought of his mother, but of all the people watching. "Oh, Lord, Pat," she groaned. "What will everyone think?" She buried her face in his chest, too embarrassed to look around her.

"They'll think I'm the luckiest man in the world," he said, hugging her. His love was in his hands and in his voice. "But I guess I ought to tell you they missed most of the show. They snuck out about the time you were giving me your dowry."

She lifted her head slightly and peeked around him. They were alone. "Thank goodness."

She backed away slightly and saw the condition of the room. Stars were scattered on the desktops, under the tables. Suns were amid the papers and on the chairs. Moons were everywhere the stars and suns weren't. "What a mess!"

Pat's embrace was sheltering and safe. "Oh, I don't know about that," he said. "It's looks to me like the view from heaven."

THE EDITOR'S CORNER

We've received thousands of wonderful letters chock-ablock with delightful, helpful comments and excellent questions and—*help!*—there is no way I can respond personally. (I assure you, though, that I have read every single note and letter that has come in.) Here, then, I'll try to answer a few of the most frequently asked questions.

First, I must apologize most sincerely for apparently misleading you by asking the question about publishing more books each month. We have *no* plans to do so during 1986. Indeed, our publishing schedule is set for the rest of the year at four books per month, and I'm really sorry for raising the hopes of so many of you for more LOVESWEPTs.

Hundreds have asked for the addresses of favorite authors. We don't give out this information, but we do forward letters. It means a lot to an author (as it does to those of us on the LOVESWEPT staff) to know that you enjoy a book, so do write. Simply send your letter to the author in care of LOVESWEPT, Bantam Books, at the address below. We love playing Post Office!

Thank you for your generous comments about the author's autobiographical sketches and about the Editor's Corner. And, by popular request (demand, really), here are the coming attractions from LOVESWEPT for the next six months!

APRIL 1986
#135—STUBBORN CINDERELLA
    by *Eugenia Riley*
#137—TARNISHED ARMOR
    by *Peggy Webb*

#136—THE RANA LOOK
    by *Sandra Brown*
#138—THE EAGLE CATCHER
    by *Joan Elliott Pickart*

MAY 1986
#139—DELILAH'S WEAKNESS
    by *Kathleen Creighton*
#141—CRESCENDO
    by *Adrienne Staff and Sally
    Goldenbaum*

#140—FIRE IN THE RAIN
    by *Fayrene Preston*
#142—TROUBLE IN TRIPLICATE
    by *Barbara Boswell*

(continued)

For this peek into the future we pay the price of very brief comments about next month's romances. Alas!

In **STUBBORN CINDERELLA** (isn't that a terrific title?) by Eugenia Riley, two extremely winning people meet in the most unlikely romantic spot—the supermarket—and it's spontaneous combustion from the start! But, heroine Tracy has only just begun to assert her independence and isn't ready to settle down. Only a Prince Charming of a hero like Anthony Delano could divert this stubborn lady from her plan . . . and you'll relish the way he goes about it.

THE RANA LOOK by Sandra Brown certainly will catch your eye on the racks next month! You'll see Sandra herself as heroine Rana and McLean Stevenson, host of the afternoon television program AMERICA, as hero Trent. The behind-the-scenes story for those of you who missed the broadcast last October, is that Sandra was flown to Los Angeles to appear on

(continued)

the program and show how a cover for a LOVESWEPT is conceived and executed. McLean really wanted to get into the character for the photographic session that leads to the final (painted) cover art. Sandra's advice to him? "Just remember that my hero Trent Gamblin is a quarterback and is used to calling all the plays . . . on *and off* the field!" She reports that McLean's sense of humor nearly got the better of her during their "clench" for this cover. By the way, the story is the sort of shimmeringly sensual and heart-warming romance you've come to expect from Sandra.

Peggy Webb gives us that most exciting sort of hero in her next LOVESWEPT—a knight in slightly **TARNISHED ARMOR**. Lance is a gorgeous male specimen who knocks prim and proper Miss Alice Spencer right off her feet. But he's also a ramblin' man while she's a homebody . . . and it seems that only a miracle can help them reconcile their differences!

Jace Dalton got his nickname—**THE EAGLE CATCHER**—from an American Indian comrade in the Air Force. But he needs more than the courage that admiring nickname indicates he's shown as a test pilot to win Heather Wade's trust . . . for she lost her young husband in a fiery crash. With courage and humor, Heather and Jace must battle a ghostly shadow to realize true and lasting love.

Again, thank you for your wonderful responses to our questionnaire!

Sincerely,

Carolyn Nichols

Carolyn Nichols
  Editor
LOVESWEPT
Bantam Books, Inc.
666 Fifth Avenue
New York, NY 10103

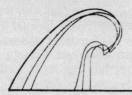

LOVESWEPT

*Love Stories you'll never forget
by authors you'll always remember*